DYING FOR DEATH

THE STUNTMAN & THE SCRIBE

HOLLY ROBERDS

**Editors: Theresa Paolo, Athena Franks, & The Havoc Archives
Sensitivity & Proof Readers: The Havoc Archives**

BOOKS BY HOLLY ROBERDS

<u>VEGAS IMMORTALS</u>

Death and the Last Vampire

Book 1 - Bitten by Death

Book 2 - Kissed by Death

Book 3 - Seduced by Death

The Beast & the Badass

Book 1 - Breaking the Beast

Book 2 - Claiming the Beast

The Stuntman & the Scribe

Book 1 - Dying For Death

<u>MONSTER UNDER MY BED</u>

Book 1 - Volume 1

<u>LOST GIRLS SERIES</u>

Book 1 - Tasting Red

Book 2 - Chasing Goldie

Book 3 - Igniting Cinder

Book 3.5 - Hooking Tink

Book 4 - Blackmailing Belle

Book 5 - Feeding Beauty

Book 6 - Tracking Snow

DEMON KNIGHTS

Book 1 - One Savage Knight

Book 2 - One Bad Knight

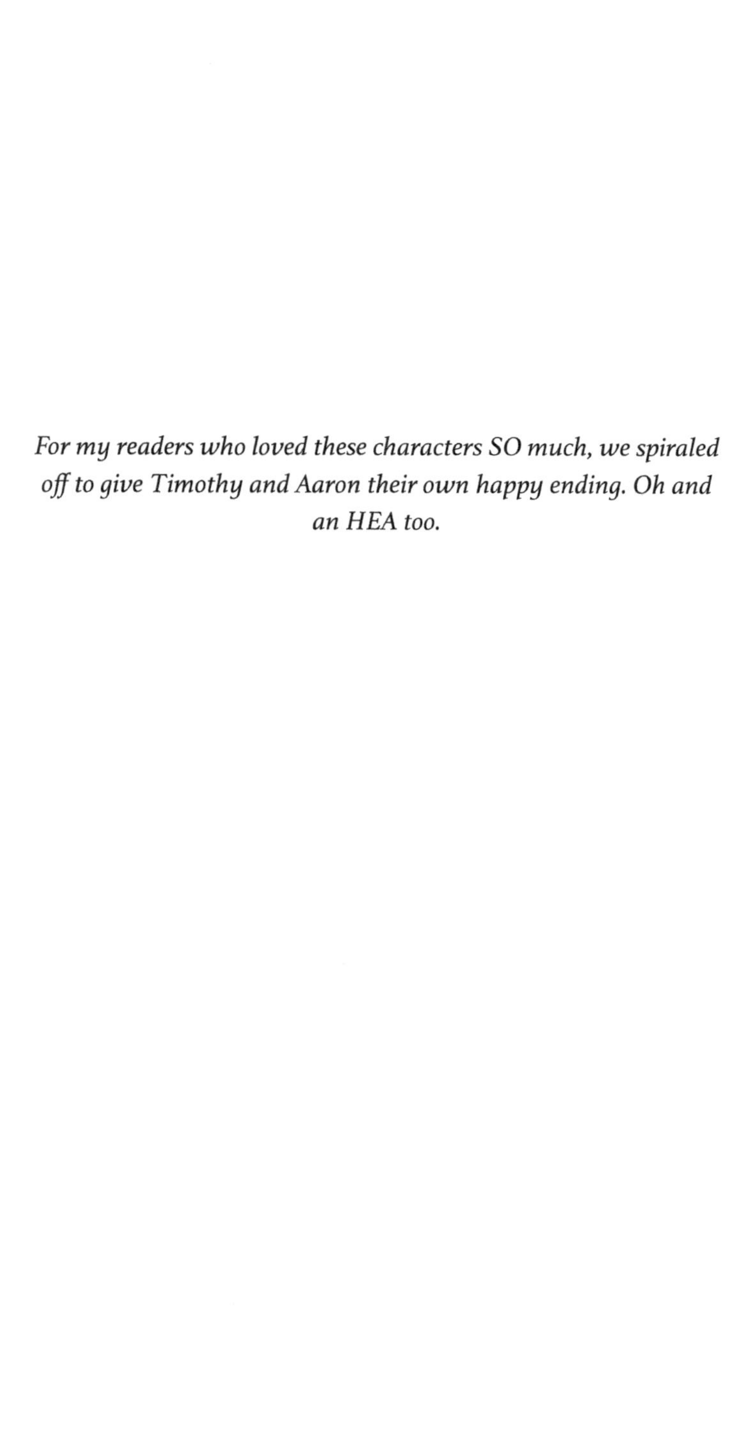

For my readers who loved these characters SO much, we spiraled off to give Timothy and Aaron their own happy ending. Oh and an HEA too.

ONE NIGHT WITH A GOD

AARON

I was taking my barista Perkatory apron off, rolling my broad shoulders back as I half listened to my coworker talk about some guy who had tipped her a hundred bucks yesterday, when heat prickled across the back of my neck. The sensation spread down my arms, tightening the muscles there, an automatic response to whenever *he* was near.

I glanced up, and sure enough, there he was but as I'd never seen him.

Timothy stood at the counter as if he'd just walked through a storm. Tie loose. Top buttons undone. Textured black hair raked out of place. His Chinese features were carved by exhaustion—cheekbones sharper than usual, eyes hard, jaw set with some emotion I couldn't identify. The clean-cut precision of him was fraying at the edges.

Timothy's dark eyes locked onto mine and the Sinopolis hotel vanished around us, the clink of cups and the distant casino noise dropping out like a switch had flipped.

His pupils expanded, and a punch rammed straight through my ribs.

I sucked in a breath, feeling my heartbeat thrum through my entire body with a new force.

I hated how hard it hit me. How fast it sank low in my gut, then climbed higher, then spread everywhere. Want. Need. The kind of pull I had spent years swallowing because he'd always kept me at arm's length.

But something had happened. Something bad. And now he was here to see me, and I couldn't resist the urge to catch him in whatever free fall this was. Though of all days, today was the exact day I should resist his pull.

Timothy was always so contained, lacquered over with impossible grace, that seeing him this unkempt felt forbidden. My chest tightened and lust hit hard enough to short circuit the rest of my brain.

I wanted, *fuck*, I wanted something I had no right to want.

Not just his attention, but to be the reason for the mess. To be the reason for that wild look, like someone had knocked the wind out of him and he still hadn't caught his breath.

My coworker's voice trailed off as I stepped around the cafe stand. I kept the balled-up apron in my hand, hiding the stiffness pressing behind my board shorts.

I stopped barely a foot away. Close enough that his heat bled into my space. Close enough to see the shadows under his eyes, the tension in his jaw.

"A-are you okay?" The question came out rougher than I'd intended. My stutter caught as my emotions neared a boiling point with him so close. Normally my speech impediment calmed when he was around, but right now I felt as on edge as he looked.

I'd finished my shift already, but I'd gladly walk back

there and make another drink if it gave me another couple minutes with him.

Damn, I was desperate.

My fingers tingled in anticipation of sneaking in a touch, as I passed him his drink.

It'd be the last time I ever got to sneak one in.

He pursed his lips and gave me a stiff nod. Finally, he spoke. "Godly business."

Right.

The fact Timothy was so far out of my league he was in a different stratosphere never stopped me from wanting to scale those heights.

Learning he was a literal god who not only dealt with coordinating the ongoings of this entire hotel but also faced down supernatural threats I hadn't known existed until a year ago should have put me back in my place.

It didn't.

When I first came to Vegas, I was just a surfer boy from California chasing the next high. While the partying had been a bonus, it had mainly been about rock climbing and seeking the next adrenaline rush. Now the only high I was interested in was climbing onto Timothy's pedestal and bringing him to his knees until he forgot his own damn name.

He shifted his weight from one foot to the other.

This would usually be the end of it. A polite check-in, a cappuccino, a safe distance, the usual. But the way his gaze dragged down my throat and back up, told me none of this was the usual. Not tonight.

Right now, he was staring at me like all the rules had been swept off the board.

He stepped closer, his voice dropping to a raw husk. "Come with me."

TIMOTHY'S private floor at Sinopolis was silent, the kind of quiet money buys. Inside his apartment, the door clicked shut and the darkness swallowed us.

Timothy's mouth crashed into mine. His tongue forced sweet heat into my mouth, rasping over my teeth. I ripped my shirt off. He thrust his hands through my sun-bleached hair, possessively yanking my head back to lick and suck at my neck, sending a burst of excited sparks down my spine and straight to my groin. Wet, ugly gasps filled the air as he bit down, the only other sound the blood rushing in my ears.

Of all days for him to lose control, it had to be this one.

I got his clothes off in quick, rough motions, until he was stripped down.His lips parted as if he couldn't decide between a command and a plea.

Those long fingers slid through my hair and along my jaw. His thumb paused at the corner of my mouth. His eyes shut hard for a beat, jaw locking as he swallowed. When he opened them again there was pain there, like touching me hurt. In his eyes I found that quiet, enduring loneliness that made my chest ache.

He didn't know I'd finished my last shift tonight. That a ticket sat in my inbox with my name on it.

My heart beat hard, loud, stupid. To an immortal like him, it probably sounded like a countdown.

If there was a way to make this body last, I would take it. I wouldn't ask what it cost.

Even as he leaned in, kissing me again, his lips trembled with the effort of restraint. Like he was afraid of breaking me. Behind his kiss lurked something powerful. I wanted him to let go completely, to let that all he was flay the skin from my bones, so the morning wouldn't come.

Tomorrow the rules would snap back into place, not because he didn't want me, but because he did. Timothy lived with a loneliness that never left him, even when he looked untouchable. If he let himself love me, he'd lose me.

That was the only ending a god got with a human. And I would be the one who made that loneliness a hundred times sharper.

I wanted to hate him for it. Tried to. But each time fury rose in me, it collapsed under the weight of understanding. I'd scream at him in my mind. Take a chance, Timothy, squeeze every drop from my short life.

Then I'd envision him a century from now, carrying my memory like another ghost he couldn't shake. And that hurt worse than his rejection.

His defenses were down right now, but this night changed nothing. So, I would take what he was offering while I could.

Scraps.

I drove him into the wall and dropped to my knees.

The first taste of him hit hot and intimate, too much and not enough. Timothy hissed and grabbed my hair. His breath broke, then broke again, and it thrilled me in the worst way.

I worked him with a hunger that had been building for years. I took what he gave and asked for more with my mouth, with my hands, with the steady pressure of my grip. My fingers slid lower and toyed with him, then cupped him, controlled the rhythm. His body tightened under my hand. His hips bucked.

"If you don't stop, I'll..." His voice fractured on the edge of it.

I didn't stop.

He may be a god, but I was in control right now. He'd handed it over to me, for once.

"Aaron." He dragged my name out.

His orgasm hit fast. His knees went unsteady. I stayed there and swallowed everything, feeling each pulse against my tongue. Salt, hot desert sand, and time itself flooded my mouth. Ancient power pressed in, and I took every last bit.

I held him until the tremors eased, until his grip loosened in my hair like the fight drained out of him.

Then I stood.

He came to me without resistance. We hit the bed and kissed hard, grabbing and groping to keep reality away. Timothy tasted like everything I never knew I needed.

I lived for adrenaline. The drop, the rush, the moment right before impact when the body decided it would survive or it wouldn't. This was worse. Better. The biggest high I'd ever touched, and I already knew the biggest crash was coming.

His legs went up not long after, his need obvious in every tight breath. I nudged against him and he made a sound that tightened my grip on him. He handed me lube with hands that weren't quite steady. His eyes tracked my face, searching, measuring, as if he could control this by watching it.

I slicked us up and pushed in.

We both groaned at the first slide. I worked deeper slowly, watching him the whole time, reading every shift in his expression, every catch of breath. He didn't look away. He took more, demanded more with the tension in his body and the hunger in his eyes.

He wanted this.

He wanted me.

And I took it, because I couldn't do anything else. Because the moment was here, because he was here, because tomorrow would bring reality back, and I would be left with nothing but the taste of him and the ache.

I rode the high. I took everything he gave, knowing it wouldn't be enough.

By morning, I'd be gone. And Timothy would still be here in a hundred years, exactly where I left him.

1

TIMOTHY

"Am I dead?" he asked.

The ghostly visage of blond beachy waves and a muscular build hit me like a punch to the chest. I couldn't breathe.

"Aaron?" The name escaped my mouth before I could bite it back. Suddenly, I was boiling in my tailored suit. My skin itched all over.

The spirit of the man in front of me looked at me with confusion and fear, then scanned the room as if in search for something familiar.

The sand-filled antechamber was lined with columns that bloomed at the top like flowers, their shafts covered in Egyptian hieroglyphics. It felt like a step into Ancient Egypt, an illusion hidden miles below the Sinopolis hotel.

I looked closer as the initial spike of adrenaline eased at seeing the man who had left Las Vegas three years, ten months, twenty-two days, and approximately eighteen minutes ago.

Loosening my tie ever so slightly, I reminded myself that,

as the scribe and recordkeeper, it only made sense to have such a keen sense of the passage of time.

Instead of bright aquamarine eyes, I was met with a dull green. Whenever Aaron had been pensive, a line pulled between his brows. This man's forehead wrinkled in concentration, and the similarities fell away.

Not Aaron.

But the deceased man in front of me bore a striking resemblance to the man I lov—

I stopped midsentence in my own head, cutting off the word I'd been about to form.

Immediately editing, revising, I took control of the narrative.

The man I had *strong* feelings for, and one night of passion.

I have to taste you.

A hot shiver ran through me at the memory of both the rasp of his words and his scruff against my skin before it settled into a cold, empty pit that seemed to have developed in my stomach nearly four years ago.

I hadn't realized how starved I was for the shape of Aaron until I saw it on another man.

"You are indeed dead." I rose from the seat on the dais, straightened my tie, and slid a hand down my suit. "And you have skated the thin edge of a life well lived and one of destruction, which is why you are now here, Mr. Morris."

His eyes traveled past mine, falling on the elaborate ancient paintings of the Egyptian god of the dead, Anubis.

In the mural, the jackal-headed god weighed a soul against the feather of Ma'at, deciding whether the man before him would be sent to the jaws of Amit to perish or cross to the Afterlife for an eternity in paradise.

Mortals had spent centuries calling him the Grim

Reaper, weaving him into fables and cautionary tales until he adopted the name, feeling it aptly earned.

Grim wasn't here to judge this soul.

That duty now fell to me. Mortals didn't whisper my name with the same fear. The world called me Timothy now, which lacked the gravitas of Thoth, God of Wisdom and Recordkeeping, but blended better in the modern world.

"You have been in the chambers with me, reaping souls since the beginning of time," Anubis said as he clapped a hand on my shoulder. *"There is no one I trust more to keep the balance, Thoth. While I'm away, keep the order. I have complete faith the souls of this world are in the best hands."*

Grim entrusted me with the scales, and I carried that weight without hesitation. It was my duty to keep the balance, and I had no intention of failing at it.

Even if the work pressed harder each day. Even if the silence of these chambers felt heavy without him.

Order required strength. I would be strong.

Suppressing a grimace, I pulled up my sleeve to reveal a tattoo of a feather. The outline lit up with blue power as it peeled away from my skin, forming into a three-dimensional object I plucked up with my other hand.

"Hey, man." James Morris threw his hands up in defense, eyes wild at the display of my power. "I'm a good dude."

"That is yet to be determined, but we'll soon know." My words were flat to my own ears, even as I reached down into his chest and pulled out his heart. Mr. Morris patted frantically at himself, searching for holes or broken ribs.

"No need to worry about your body anymore, Mr. Morris. You shed the mortal form when you foolishly decided to illegally bungee jump off the Hoover Dam." I had to suppress an eye roll.

"Whoa, that's how I died?" His face brightened. "Oh man, that's the way to go. I bet so many chicks will be so sad they won't get to bang me after that, but I bet they cry."

This time I didn't suppress the eye roll.

What an absolute gem of a mortal.

Definitely not Aaron.

He would have stuttered at least once by now, a side effect from being hit in the jugular by a surfboard. Though admittedly I could easily believe Aaron to be foolish enough to try and pull off the same kind of stunt as Mr. Morris here.

The man's heart and the feather traveled behind me to the wall with the massive painting of scales. The feather and heart settled on either scale and the entire painting glowed blue as I fed it my magic.

The scales rocked up and down, to and fro, before landing decidedly. The heart side raised high.

"It seems as though your stupidity and selfish deeds have not tainted your heart. Looks like your soul will not make a meal for Amit today."

His nose scrunched. "What's an Amit?"

"A crocodile god who eats souls," I explained, before giving into the extreme urge and pulling out my tablet from where it was wedged in my seat on the dais.

"But no, your fate, Mr. Morris, lies in the glorious After-life where Hraf-Hraf will ferry you into the waiting arms of Osiris, who will deliver you to your Eden."

Mr. Morris's shoulders tightened as he shifted from foot to foot. "Who and who?"

Instead of answering, I sat down before meeting his gaze. "You'll see."

The scales dissolved along with the wall, opening up to a

vista with a beautiful blue sky that expanded over thick, lush green reeds.

The vast landscape sucked Mr. Morris into it then rearranged itself into painted sandstone, the picture of the scales back in place. A slight tingling on my arm told me the feather of Ma'at had resumed its place.

The chamber was deathly quiet in the wake of his crossing.

Despite having turned on my tablet to distract myself with whatever organizational task was closest at hand, I found myself staring at the screen without seeing.

It wasn't him, my mind reassured me.

But one day it might be. Or maybe I just wished it?

Could Aaron have tainted his soul enough in three years to warrant judgment before passing into the Afterlife?

If he did, it would mean I'd get to see him one more time. He'd appear before me, right in this chamber.

Or you could find him now and just call, a practical if not sassy voice in my head retorted. It sounded too much like the voices of my friends, Vivian and Miranda, braided into one.

Was he still in Costa Rica? All it would take was his name and a thought. I could pull Aaron's file, trace the thread of his soul wherever it wandered on earth, tilt the ledgers of eternity a fraction in my favor. One tiny misuse of power. One tiny crack in the rules.

I told him we could never be, and he listened.

Everything ended for the best. A relationship between a god and a mortal was a recipe for chaos and heartbreak, of which I was interested in neither.

A whine from nearby pulled my attention. A reaper dog set its head on my knee, looking up at me with glowing gold eyes that were filled with concern. My heart clenched. The reaper was intuiting my emotions again. This one had been doing so regularly. And a whine from the animal now made me aware of the emotions I had been trying to ignore.

I lifted a hand to stroke its glossy black coat. The tension inside me eased ever so slightly as my fingers met with the soft, plush fur of my self-appointed companion.

It had been such a brief moment between us, yet nearly four years had done nothing to soften the sting of Aaron's absence. Some centuries seemed to slip by in an instant, but each year since that night passed in a slow, torturous crawl.

While time had always been something I tracked and recorded to keep order since the dawn of mortals, it now felt like a punishment.

What would have happened if we'd had more than a single night?

A year?

An entire mortal lifetime?

I was certain I would never be able to recover after Aaron's final passing. Not even after millennia.

Now, I was starting to believe I wouldn't ever be released from his hold, even after spending only a single night with him.

The thought settled, heavy and useless.

For a fleeting moment, I considered ending my day there. Closing the chamber. Leaving the rest of the docket for tomorrow. I had already judged dozens of souls today.

But order did not bend for exhaustion, and balance did not care about the heaviness in my chest. I straightened and continued. Longing had no place in the work before me.

I gave the reaper another pet of assurance. "Enough of that, Assirak. I'll never see him again, and we have much work to do."

2

TIMOTHY

My heart still raced with anticipation as I stepped up to the counter of Perkatory after yet another long day of judgment. The lobby around me hummed with its usual low, controlled energy. Unlike the chaotic crush of other Vegas hotels, Sinopolis held a curated stillness.

The black onyx floors gleamed like wet volcanic sand from the old Egyptian shores, reflecting the warm gold lights in ripples. Tall palms framed the space, their trunks carved to mimic ancient oasis groves, the faint scent of lotus blossoms drifting from the vents.

The strong, fresh espresso overpowered my senses at the cafe, curling through the air, tightening my gut.

This counter used to be *his* station. The place where Aaron handed me coffee in a way that ensured our fingers would brush or become entwined for seconds that somehow both lasted for eons and ended in a blink, leaving me breathless. My skin prickled, still feeling the hot intensity of his gaze boring into me until I squirmed under it. Then he'd smile as if he'd won some kind of prize.

My pulse spiked. I kept my expression composed, unwilling to be undone by the simple routine action of getting a coffee.

"May I have a double espresso?" Assirak pawed my leg in reminder from where he sat dutifully at my feet. "Oh, and a pup cup," I added.

Before the barista could find the button, a familiar voice cut in. "Make that a triple. You're going to need it."

Miranda strode toward me, box braids swinging, the sword at her hip humming with irritated energy. The human sword-wielder would never interrupt a break for caffeine unless something was very wrong.

"Miranda," I greeted, even as the girl behind me loudly ground the beans for my elixir of life.

"Timothy." She gave me a quick grin that didn't reach her eyes. Something was definitely wrong. "You've been hiding in the basement for too long."

"I call it working," I said dryly.

"Semantics." She waved a dismissive hand. "Drink fast. You need to come outside. That dick pickle is causing a ruckus. The asshole is up to something."

I didn't need clarification on who Miranda thought was a dick pickle. Seth had returned to Las Vegas a couple weeks prior, reclaiming control of his hotel. Last week, he'd thrown a party, so loud and raucous that it boomed down the entire Strip all night. The extravagance with which he seemed to be celebrating his return didn't bode well.

My pulse ticked up, an unwelcome reminder that even gods had nervous systems. I grabbed the small cup, threw the hot, bitter liquid back, adjusted my cufflinks, then followed Miranda through the lobby and outside. Assirak trotted by my side, dutifully. I waited until we were out of view of the barista to hold out the pup cup for him. He lapped up the sweetness in two large licks.

We stepped through the glass doors onto the street. The slanted lines of Sinopolis blazed with a gold light in the heavy desert night.

The air was alive, electric, hot, the Strip packed shoulder to shoulder with humans. Anticipation buzzed through the crowd, a live wire.

"There he is." I nudged Miranda, so she'd follow my gaze.

Seth stood on a dais he'd erected in the middle of the crowd, like he was a king among peasants.

What was he up to? Why leave the Menaggio and come to Sinopolis to create a fuss?

The gleaming white of his charming smile matched his immaculate suit, both blinding under the Strip's neon glow —a predator's display of perfect teeth behind lips curled in practiced charisma. The black shirt beneath his jacket was open at the throat in a way that broadcasted money, leisure, and zero consequences.

Salt-and-pepper hair slicked back over a deeply tanned face. Martini in hand, he smiled broadly as phones went up around him, reveling in the attention.

Seth already had a following on social media before gods were revealed to the public. Humans had been idolizing us for years without realizing what we were, or that we ruled the hotels along the Vegas Strip.

Miranda's voice was low but sharp. "You'd think being decapitated and trapped inside Bob for a couple of years would've taught him some humility."

The sword pulsed faintly at her side, a low, metallic thrum. Bob, or the Blade of Bane, was the only weapon that could kill immortals. Or rather, contain them within its steel, imprisoning them. Miranda may be human, but she was worthy to carry it and hear it speak in her mind.

I glanced at it. "What did he say?"

"Bob remembers the taste of him," she said, her mouth a grim line. "And he doesn't want seconds."

I cut through the crowd, Miranda close behind, and Assirak on my heels. We stopped at the velvet rope where guards held everyone back from the platform.

"Quite the turnout," Seth said as he caught sight of us, voice carrying easily over the crowd. "You'd think the people of Vegas were starved for a little fun."

The bouncer unhooked the rope and let us through.

"What do you think you are doing?" I asked with open annoyance. "This isn't something you could have done at your hotel?"

His eyes flicked to the light streaming out of the top of the pyramid and piercing the sky. His smile widened, naked lust and greed in his expression.

My body and powers prickled with warning. Seth, the god of chaos, had always been hungry for power. Angling to take the mantle of God of the Dead so he could be in control of the souls, the balance, and the rest of the gods.

Miranda didn't bother hiding her scowl. "What are you doing, Seth? Trying to amass people to worship you? You know what happens if you draw too much power." She shifts Bob so the Vegas lights bounce and glint off his sharp edge.

Seth chuckled darkly, as if remembering his last encounter with the Blade of Bane all too well. Seth sipped at his martini before throwing her an overly congenial smile. "Followers? Don't be absurd. This is entertainment. A celebration for the mortals, for the world. A reminder that the gods among them can give them wonder."

"You mean, a reminder that you can," she said. "If you start to tip the balance, I'll stop you myself."

A part of me couldn't help but think I should threaten Seth to stay in line. It's what Grim would have done. But that had never been my style. I was far more surgical in my approach to things. My power was in details, in precision, in knowing the rules better than anyone and finding the loopholes then closing them. I simply needed to wait and watch to figure out what Seth was up to and then I'd set to motion. And that motion may very well be holding Seth down while Miranda cut off his head.

My mouth tightened at the thought. Unpleasant, but potentially necessary.

Seth opened his arms. "Is this any way to treat someone who thought of you, all lonely at this big hotel, covering somebody else's job? How long has it been since Grim and Vivian left our plane for the Afterlife at the behest of Osiris?"

"You know damn well it's been four months," Miranda said between gritted teeth.

"Four already?" Seth tutted. "You must be exhausted covering for Grim."

"I'm doing just fine," I said flatly.

Seth shrugged a shoulder, looking off into the crowd with feigned indifference. "Well, if you should ever need help—"

"I am more than capable," I interrupted with more edge in my voice. He's not interested in helping anyone other than himself.

Specifically, to the power of all the mortal souls the God of the Dead wields. All the gods are in Vegas to be warmed and powered by the hub where souls pass through for judgment. The further a god got from the well of souls and the doorway to the Afterlife, the weaker they felt.

Like a dysfunctional, co-dependent family, all the gods did our best to keep our distance from each other while being practically stacked on top of each other.

Controlling the souls and the doorway to the Afterlife made Grim the most powerful of us on this mortal plane—that is, until he passed the mantle to me.

Along with a massive influx of magic, the position came with a large target painted on my back. I'd never felt it so openly as now.

Seth let out a lofty laugh. "Of course you are. But I still feel compelled to help ease your burden. Oh, do you hear that? The show is about to start. Would you like a cocktail, or perhaps a leash so your pet doesn't do anything rash?" The last part he practically spat out.

Assirak growled, because we both knew he meant Miranda.

She lifted the sword to pass over her face, a dark, manic gleam in her eye. "Come try it, big boy."

Seth sipped his drink, though I noticed his body tense. He'd never admit to being afraid of a human. Yet, he was, just a little. He'd been trapped in Bob before. He wasn't keen to be cut down and imprisoned again.

Spotlights streaked up the pyramid as the neighboring hotels and streetlights went dark. A roar of excited screams filled the air with anticipation.

The thrum of helicopter blades split the night.

Seth sipped his martini. "Let's give Vegas what it came for."

The powerful rotors drowned out the crowd. A helicopter descended through the fireworks, dragging a steel platform on cables. The crowd erupted as the lights locked onto the descending shape. At its center sat a motorcycle, black chrome blazing under the glare.

A lone man straddled it. Helmeted. Black leather pants. A simple black tee stretched across broad shoulders.

Against all the steel and glass, all the machinery and spectacle, he looked painfully vulnerable. Flesh and muscle dangling over a city built of metal and gods.

Even from this distance, there was something about him...Perhaps it was the lighting, but I could almost swear I could see a kind of glow emanating around him.

An announcer's voice boomed over the Strip. "Ladies and gentlemen, courtesy of Seth and Sinopolis, we welcome you to The Pyramid Plunge!"

Miranda frowned. "Tell me that guy isn't going to do what I think he's going to do."

The helicopter adjusted its angle, lowering the platform just above the peak of the pyramid.

It took several long moments to steady above the lit apex. The stuntman didn't move even as the entire city seemed to hold its breath.

I stared at the helmeted figure, breath shallow. Sweat broke out along my spine. That man was going to die. No human could do this stunt.

"Seth," I practically barked. "Call it off. I don't know how you compelled this man to do something so suicidal. People are going to get hurt."

My brain raced, calculating all the calamities about to happen. The glass of the hotel breaking under the impact of the motorcycle. The screams of people watching him slide and crash to his death before steel and glass debris rained on the crowd of vulnerable humans. My hands fisted into balls.

"Seth. Stop this now." I demanded when he didn't move.

"Pfft, lighten up, Thoth," Seth said, downing the last of his martini in a final swallow.

The spotlight followed the rider as the platform dipped slightly. The rider revved the engine and leaned forward. The sound was pure thunder rolling down the Strip.

"Oh, sweet baby Jesus," Miranda muttered with the same fear and trepidation.

The next instant, he drove straight off the edge. The platform fell away and the bike launched into nothing, a dark shape arcing against the lights as panic ripped through the crowd. Screams filled the air.

My breath caught in my chest as my mind raced for a way to reach him with my power to save him or those below, but I was too far away.

The bike dropped several stories before its tires hit the pyramid's face. The building didn't give way. Instead, sparks showered from the contact as he raced down the slanted glass.

"He's insane," Miranda said under her breath.

Seth smiled without looking away. "He's fearless. Vegas deserves nothing less."

Halfway down, the rider launched off one of the lower ridges and the crowd inhaled as a collective, breath snagging as man and machine free-fell before slamming down near the base and tearing onward across the marble forecourt, tires screaming and smoke boiling in his wake. He spun in a perfect arc and came to a stop in the center of the Sinopolis emblem.

The lights cut out, plunging the plaza into sudden darkness. Only the rumble of the engine filled the silence.

For a breathless beat, no one moved. Then the spotlights snapped back on, and the rider sat motionless, head bowed, and the penned-in masses lost control. Shouts burst free, hands slammed against steel rails, bodies pressed forward in a heaving crush.

One wave broke toward the fallen rider, voices rising in frantic awe, while the closer press peeled back toward the dais, crashing in around us. Heat, sound, and motion rolled through me at once as they screamed their enthusiasm to the conductor of the entire event. Seth.

The god next to me waved to the cheering masses with a smug grin.

Something sharp lanced through my chest. Seth took the hotel I was in charge of and made it his personal playground. It wasn't about the stunt. It was about firmly putting two feet into my territory and pissing in the sand.

I wasn't the only one who noticed.

Miranda took a step closer to Seth, her grip tightening around her sword.

"Miranda," I said in warning. Her gaze locked on mine, and words passed between us without either of us uttering a single one.

Back down.

I don't like it, Timothy. Something's off about this.

I agree, but there's nothing we can do right now.

Miranda stepped away, lowering Bob with great reluctance.

My attention locked on the stuntman in the spotlight. Something in the tilt of his head, the wave of his arm, crawled under my skin. But the glow around him confirmed something I suspected as he rode down Sinopolis.

He wasn't human.

"I think you two deserve to meet the daredevil of the hour," Seth said. "I'll be just a moment." With that, he disappeared down the stairs, flanked by his guards.

"This feels an awful lot like he's getting people to

worship him," Miranda said, glaring after him. "Drawing power he's not supposed to."

"I agree, but I don't sense any swell of power. This isn't worship, and they seem more likely to fall at the feet of that stuntman. But he is trying to undermine my authority by performing this stunt on my turf."

"So kick his ass, put him back in his place," Miranda pitched.

I shook my head. "I can't. Technically, he's broken no rules."

"Timothy," she said with open exasperation, "sometimes the rules aren't as important as the effect. Don't let that dick pickle by on a technicality. You have to rule the other gods here, and he just made a clear move against you."

Boots thudded on the platform as the rider joined us, though Seth was nowhere in sight. My next words died on my tongue.

The rider tugged his helmet off, and blood roared in my ears. My heart did a sick, skipping hiccup that left an ache in my sternum while my mouth instantly dried.

Aaron ran a gloved hand through his hair. It tumbled out in golden waves, sweat-dark and longer than I remembered. The precise cut of his jaw, the crook in his nose, and the glint of mischief in his smile were so beautiful it physically hurt to look at.

"Miss me?" he asked.

Shock hit first, sharp and breath-stealing, and then the want followed, heavy and disorienting. My chest locked, my pulse tripped over itself, and a cold awareness slid through me as my body reacted faster than thought.

Not only because the man I woke up and fell asleep thinking about was in front of me. This close, the crystallized glow surrounding him was painfully obvious.

Aaron's soul was no longer a fluid, transient energy. It had hardened like a diamond. Frozen and preserved for all eternity in a body nearly just as indestructible.

The truth detonated within me like a bomb. The shock and horror of his transformation rippled through my frame, threatening to bend my bones.

Aaron was a vampire.

3

AARON

I wished Timothy had looked at least slightly less beautiful than the last time I saw him. But unfortunately, my vampire senses betrayed me.

My new eyes soaked in every perfect detail in high definition. Not a single pore visible, not one hair out of place unless he wanted it to be. Each angle of his East Asian features carved by a divine hand, the symmetry of his face was the kind of perfection artists spend lifetimes trying to capture. Even the air around him seemed clearer, more vibrant. It seemed I was seeing reality itself bend slightly to accommodate his divine presence.

It made me want to stick my fingers in his perfectly tousled, gelled hair and mess it up, just to see his cheeks heat with red. The full, dark lashes slanting down over his eyes were so full they'd make any woman envious. And while his lips were thin, a sign he was caught in deep thought, I still remembered them turning pliant and soft under my mouth.

Standing this close, the scent of sandalwood and his skin filled my senses, and I was transported back to his bedroom.

Back to when I breathed him in while tracing my tongue along his throat, as his hand encircled my hard length, as my every dream and desire played out in real time.

Calm down, cowboy, I sternly reminded myself. These tight pants won't cover up a stiffy all that well.

The black dog at Timothy's side pushed its head under his hand, but he didn't seem to notice the nudge.

When did Mr. Control Freak himself get a cute pooch?

"You should see your face," I said with the satisfaction of being able to surprise a god.

"Holy shit, Aaron," Miranda said, also dumbfounded with shock.

I ran my fingers through my hair, deliberately relaxing my shoulders, pretending to play it cool.

But how could I really be chill about this?

Not while the god I fell head over heels with years ago stood a couple feet from me, looking perfectly coiffed, but with an expression of someone who'd slapped him across the face with a dead fish.

Miranda slammed into me in a full-body hug. I stiffened on instinct, because the Miranda I remembered barely tolerated pats on the back. Before I got my arms to cooperate, she pulled away and drove a fist into my shoulder. Hard.

"Ow," I said for effect because it felt more like the impact of a gnat. My strength was beyond anything I'd imagined it could be now.

"You're back in town and you don't text me, you jackass?" Miranda tilted her chin up with barely veiled accusation.

A smile played at my lips, but it fell short. My focus shifted without permission, pulled past Miranda to the presence looming behind her.

Timothy's expression had slowly but surely morphed from utter surprise to shock.

A subtle but important difference. One can only be short-lived, while the other can far outlast the first reaction.

He knew what I was. Of course, he would.

Gods and Sekhors, or what was more modernly called vampires, used to bond in ancient times. Or rather, Sekhors were enslaved by the gods.

I did my best not to shy away, not to cringe in guilt or shame. I had nothing to be guilty about. I didn't owe him anything.

Even so, an ache I'd carried at the center of my chest spread and intensified under his scrutiny.

"I've been...busy," I said to Miranda by way of explanation.

"And what the hell is wrong with you? Doing a crazy stunt like that? Have you completely lost your surfer boy mind? You could have died."

"No, he couldn't."

The answer came from Timothy. His words cold and stiff despite his innately charming British accent.

My shoulders tightened at the tone, though I tried not to let it show. The ache in my chest twisted like a knife, plunging deeper into me. The pressure of Timothy's piercing gaze made it hard to focus on anything else. The air felt thick between us, stretching each second as I grappled with the unspoken truth that he knew what I was now. A surge of anxiety washed over me, leaving me acutely aware of my own unnaturalness in this moment, and I struggled to maintain my cool under his scrutiny.

"What are you talking about?" Miranda scoffed. "You of all people should tell him not to do stupid, dangerous shit."

Timothy's jaw flexed ever so slightly.

He might as well have punched me in the gut.

Miranda's gaze volleyed between us, her brows screwed up with confusion. "What am I missing?"

"Shall you tell her, or would you like me to?"

I could have broken frozen chunks of ice off Timothy's words.

I ran my tongue along my teeth and shot an easy smile at Miranda. "I've gone through some changes since I've last seen you."

"What, like puberty?" She guffawed at her own joke, before she stilled. Her gaze caught on my smile.

Specifically, my teeth. More particularly at my elongated vampire incisors.

The humor slid right out of her expression. Her face went taut, eyes widening as her breath caught. "Aaron, how...when?"

A hand clapped my shoulder. "Ah, I see you've met my main attraction."

Seth's cultured voice slithered into my ears and wrapped around my throat like an invisible hand. I tried to maintain a smile, but it faded despite my best efforts.

"Set," Timothy said, using Seth's ancient name even as his eyes fastened to Seth's grip on my shoulder.

Miranda raised her blade, her posture stiffening, eyes narrowed.

It was only then that Timothy stepped forward. "What do you mean, this is your main attraction?"

"Well, you saw the show, didn't you?" Seth asked. "Aaron is spectacular, and he's drawing droves of people to my hotel. I'm making him into a star." His hand moved from my shoulder to a possessive hold on the back of my neck.

I'd spent the last few months doing exactly what Seth wanted and hating him for how well he understood me. He dangled heights and speed as bait and I took it every time, running Sinopolis rooftops, dropping from ledges that would have shattered my human bones, landing clean and laughing before the rush even faded. The world was bigger, now that I was a vampire. Stronger legs. Faster reflexes. No fear of the fall. I chased the thrill willingly, then looked up to find the leash still wrapped around my throat, the contracts and terms and cameras waiting to claim the moment. The rush was mine. The show piece wasn't. It made me feel...used.

There was no squelching the shame this time. I stared at Timothy, watching his reaction. Willing him to understand why I didn't come find him after I'd been turned into a vampire.

His face went through a series of minute changes—first, a tightening around his eyes, then a barely perceptible twitch at the corner of his mouth, followed by a slight flaring of his nostrils. To anyone else, he might have appeared impassive, but I could read the devastation in those subtle shifts like a book written in a language only I understood.

"He's yours." Timothy's words came out soft but flat, and my guts cliff dove right out of my stomach and smashed into the ground.

The disappointment, the pain that flashed over his features was what kept me away. Like the coward I was. Barely perceptible to anyone else, but I could read him. I always could.

It was gone in a moment, replaced with his placid face of business.

"Yes, my Sekhor, Aaron," Seth said, grinning at me. "He and I are blood-bonded."

Miranda's eyes widened, sword dropping to her side as

she clearly needed a minute, or twenty, to comprehend what Timothy had gleaned far quicker.

He was always too clever for his own good.

"He's been most...useful," Seth said, fingers massaging the back of my neck in encouragement. Then as if finally noting the tension, Seth stopped. "Though I get the sense you've all been acquainted before."

He dropped his hand, waiting for any of us to answer. A long, loaded, three beats passed.

Danger crept up my spine with warning prickles at the idea of letting Seth know too much. The god was all flash and swagger on the outside, but I knew he was always planning, leveraging, manipulating.

"Yes, he used to work for Grim at Sinopolis," Timothy supplied, as official as ever. I suppressed the urge to roll my eyes. His business-like manner was so stiff, I wondered if he hadn't turned into a robot version of himself in the last few minutes.

"Yeah," I brushed my fingers through my hair. "I worked at Perkatory cafe for a couple years."

And stayed far longer than I did anywhere else because of a certain dark-haired man who took his cappuccinos with extra foam.

"Is that so?" Seth said slowly.

He looked between us, as if trying to guess what wasn't being said. A dark eagerness flickered in his eyes, and I shifted my weight, fighting the urge to bolt.

Then Seth laughed as if he'd heard some great joke. "Well, isn't it a very, very small world?"

Timothy's gaze burned into me until my heart fluttered and flipped like a snowboarder. "The smallest."

4

TIMOTHY

The glass was cool in my hand as I looked out at the neon lights of the city. Wearing only my boxer briefs, I was still somehow hot under the collar.

I'd been overheated since seeing *him*.

My place near the top of Sinopolis was dark, but illuminated well enough by the lights from the Strip. Assirak lay on the couch behind me, watching me but giving me space. I knew he was at the ready if I needed him.

While Seth was definitely up to no good, Miranda, Assirak, and I left because we couldn't prove anything was amiss.

Seth had created an absolute spectacle and did it as a show of power.

He was up to something, and I'd no doubt he delighted in igniting my paranoia. But he couldn't have known what Aaron was to me.

And Aaron clearly didn't know about Seth, if he was foolish enough to blood-bond with the god.

"I can't believe it."

Miranda words echoed back to me from when we

stalked back into the lobby of Sinopolis while the crowd cleared. "Aaron seems the same, yet...different. I mean, his stutter is gone, but is that a vampire healing thing? More importantly, he's been here for months? What are we? Chop liver?"

"He's obviously been occupied," I had said, my words controlled, belying the way my fingers tapped against my thigh as my stomach twisted, desperate for something to hold onto. Or perhaps crush.

Miranda's hand on my arm forced me to stop so I would look at her.

"Just because they are blood-bonded, it doesn't mean they are...more."

The queasiness had turned into an all-out scalding nausea. Even now, acid rose up my throat as sweat beaded along my hairline.

Not just at the thought that Aaron had been in the city, practically under my nose for months, not just because he'd been turned, but because the flash of guilt in his eyes when Seth held him by the scruff of the neck.

As if Aaron were some kind of possession. Some kind of dog he could hold up and show off.

Seth had no more respect for vampires than he did for humans. Hell, he had no regard for anyone other than himself, god or otherwise.

I'd like to believe I'd achieved some kind of mastery over my own baser instincts, that all these years observing humans and their endless dramas had distilled in me a stoic calm, a detachment from the frantic, animal workings of passion.

But standing there, I felt the crude machinery of my anger whir to life in ways that surprised even me. The sight of Seth's hold on Aaron sent a tremor of raw, involuntary rage reverberating from the base of my skull down through my rib cage.

My vision, usually so precise and clinical, blurred at the edges. It was all I could do not to rip Seth's arm out of its socket and beat him with the wet end.

I did not, of course. But the violence of that urge still called to me in vivid fantasy.

Seth's shriek, the spray of dark blood, the look on Aaron's face when he realized that, at the end of all this, the only hands left to touch him would be mine.

I sucked in a shuddering breath, attempting to calm myself. Closing my eyes, I tried to clear the violent images I couldn't stop replaying.

I'd always ruled my emotions with the iron logic of a chess player, weighing each move, calculating the cost, the potential gain, focused on the long game. I could talk myself down from anything.

Except this.

Watching Aaron be touched—claimed, even, by anyone but me—made all that careful discipline go molten. It was as if I'd spent a century damming up a reservoir and had, in a single second, decided to blow it all to hell.

And though a blood-bond was not necessarily sexual in nature, the idea they had...that they might be...

Whipping away from the window and crossing to the dark kitchen, I gripped the edge of the kitchen counter.

I suddenly wished I had a vice I could turn to. Drinking, smoking, gambling, anything. But my only vice had ever been a blond human with sparkling turquoise eyes, a stutter, and an easy confidence that kept pulling me to that coffee shop day after day.

Shutting my eyes tight, my brain flicked through too many memories, too many emotions.

A crunch preceded the countertop giving way under my hands.

White marble bits fell from my hands, hitting the tile floor. Assirak sat up where he lay on the couch, ears alert and at attention.

"I can't do this," I said out loud to myself. "I need to stay in control. Aaron belongs to someone else. I have my duty to uphold. It's as simple as that."

Decision made, I went about doing what I did best. Cleaning up the mess.

"May I have an extra hot cappuccino?" I requested at Perkatory.

It had been another long day of judging souls. The sun had long since set, yet there was still more work to do managing the hotel and planning the Convergence. We were days from the alignment of the stars, and it was important I made a show of strength.

I needed fuel and a place to work. Preferably somewhere in the middle of a crowd where I wouldn't be noticed but could use the sweep of energy all around me to focus.

The barista fumbled with the buttons on the screen in front of her, as a red tinge flooded her cheeks. "I'm sorry, I'm new. I just need to find the button for extra hot."

"And add cinnamon," a familiar voice came from behind me.

Every nerve ending prickled with desperation and fearful hope. Heat coiled tight in my lower abdomen.

Aaron sidled up next to me, washing me in his clean ocean scent. He wore board shorts and a tank top that showed off the perfect swell of his biceps and shoulder muscles. A leather necklace adorned with a shark tooth fell to the top of his chest. For a moment, it was almost like no time had passed. Except I couldn't ignore the glow of his crystallized soul.

"He needs a dash of cinnamon on the top to remind him it's okay to go a little wild sometimes," Aaron instructed the barista with a wink, then turned his ultimate weapon on me. His thousand-watt smile.

The weight of duty and responsibility dropped away from me as a heat spread out from the center of my chest.

The world bent toward him until I could believe that everything would work out just fine as long as I stood next to this man. As long as he continued to look at me just like that.

"Can I get you anything?" I gestured to the cafe, determined not to let him see me affected.

Aaron's expression darkened. His eyes dropped to the floor as the words left his mouth, one hand rising to rub the back of his neck. "Not exactly the kind of thing I drink anymore."

My throat tightened until it nearly closed off.

Of course not. He was blood-bonded to Seth.

There was only one thing he consumed. And only one person he could drink from.

Even as I tried to block out the visions of the two of them together, jealousy roiled in the pit of my stomach.

Another reason I couldn't indulge in fantasies of Aaron. I trapped my thoughts between the unforgiving covers of a hardback tome in my mind before shelving it away at the back of my brain where I couldn't reach them. A tactic that worked, but never for long.

After I paid, we stepped aside. "I'm glad to see you," I said, proud of the businesslike manner I was able to maintain in Aaron's presence, though my entire being screamed at me to touch him.

That infuriatingly mischievous grin curved his mouth again. "Yeah? How glad?"

My entire body heated as something turned weightless in my chest.

"Glad because I need to speak with you," I clarified. "Do you have a few minutes to spare?"

Aaron shoved his hands into his pockets. "For you? I have several handfuls of minutes."

His face lit up as he spotted Assirak next to me.

"I can't believe you actually got a dog." Aaron crouched down. The reaper's mouth opened, his tongue lolling out as Aaron ruffled his ears and scratched his head, then worked his way down until reaper rolled over and Aaron attacked his exposed belly. "Who's a good boy? You're a good boy," he said in baby talk.

"A dog?" The barista said, perking up from behind the counter. "I love dogs." She rounded the corner in search of the pup, only for her face to cinch in confusion and disappointment.

It took several attempts to clear my throat to get Aaron's attention. When he finally looked up, he realized the barista was giving him the strangest look.

'You're a vampire now. You can see the reapers," I said to him under my breath.

Realization dawned on Aaron's face as his gaze swung from me to the barista who stared at what looked like empty space under his hands.

The reaper dogs fetched souls of the deceased then brought them to me for judgment. They could only be seen by Gods and Vampires.

"Oh, right," he said. While Aaron had never seen them before now, he'd known *of* them.

Aaron laughed nervously as he stood again, wiping his hands on his shorts. "Sorry," he said to the barista, "I'm practicing for my mime act later. You know, all kinds of shows happen on the Strip."

I worked to suppress a snort, failing miserably.

The sheer disappointment on her face made it seem as though he had committed an unforgivable sin by pretending there was a dog she could pet.

"Still getting used to this vamp business," Aaron muttered, falling into step with me and making a quick getaway from the girl's accusing glare.

I SAT behind the desk in my office, setting down my untouched coffee as Aaron chose to stand instead of taking the seat across from me.

Floor-to-ceiling bookcases lined the walls of my stark white sanctuary, their shelves punctuated by artificial greenery amid my alphabetized collection.

Between the volumes sat carefully arranged mementos —each positioned with the precision of chess pieces on a board.

My chair rolled smooth as silk. The armrests were cool under my fingertips. The lacquered desk reflected the faintest movement, pillar-straight pens and folders perched in precise alignment along its edge. A diffuser ran in the corner, pumping out a grounding, woody mix of cedarwood and frankincense into the space.

Where I enjoyed the familiar nostalgia of stepping back in time to our Egyptian homeland in the chambers of judgment below the hotel, I appreciated the modernity of my office. It was a refuge of order and efficiency, a pristine temple of contemporary design, where my mind could find solace and clarity amidst the chaos of the world.

Though I failed to feel that clarity with Aaron hovering over the corner of my desk. He picked up one of the pens, rolling it between his fingers.

A vivid memory of his dexterous fingers wrapping around me flashed hot and bright, hitting me right in the solar plexus.

I cleared my throat against the sudden heat building inside. "I need you to tell me what Seth is planning."

Aaron shrugged with indifference even though his clear blue eyes stayed glued to me with an unerring focus. "He's putting on a show. He's hyping me up. Making me famous, I guess." He set the pen down, askew on my desk.

The off-kilter position of it burgeoned a faint pressure that settled between my eyes.

Aaron wandered over to the bookshelves, unbothered.

I stood up and rounded my desk to pick up the errant pen and set it back in the cup with the others.

"And you *want* to be famous?" I prodded.

Aaron regarded the rows of old tomes. "I guess. It doesn't really matter much to me." He picked up a glass paperweight shaped like a pyramid then set it down on a shelf below before walking on. This time the bridge of my nose prickled with an irritation I could not explain away.

"All I really want is to feel the rush, you know what I mean? And since becoming a vampire, I can do a lot of crazy shit." He tossed me a grin over his shoulder.

Like I should be impressed with his wild death stunt habit.

The vision of his leather-clad body in that helmet

descending from the sky, straddling that bike now took on a whole new tenor in my memory.

Why did his recklessness pull at me? I could never logically understand why that part of him appealed to me. Or maybe logic wasn't part of it.

It was just...all of him. The way he'd tease me when I'd go to get my coffee from Perkatory. The grin that lit up his entire face until it felt like I was looking at the sun itself. Even when he got stuck in a stutter, he never seemed to let it bother him, and I never minded waiting until he got his bearings.

There was such warmth that rolled off him that I felt my cold immortality melt and flex underneath it, until I came alive.

That same grin now had me brusquely clearing my throat as hot tingles swept up my arms and shoulders, moving up my neck and landing in my ears, which were no doubt a bright red.

"Yes, but you don't know Seth, not like I do." I crossed over and moved the miniature pyramid back to its original spot. "He can't be trusted. He's been looking to usurp Grim since the beginning of time. I have no doubt he is up to something, and I wouldn't put it past him to use you to get what he wants."

Seth had tried to grab the power for himself over many different lifetimes. I could only assume he was attempting to try again, thinking I'd be the weak link he could tear through to get at what he wanted. Ultimate power so he could run things more to his liking.

I couldn't help but think he was using Aaron to meet those ends, though I had no idea how that would be possible. There were plenty of vampires in circulation now and their relationships with gods were carefully watched and monitored.

Or they were monitored by Vivian, before she went off with her husband, Grim, merrily into the Afterlife with her reaper companion, Cupcake.

Which meant someone needed to look into this dynamic a bit closer. That someone would have to be me.

Aaron pulled out another book, flipping through it absently. My grip tightened reflexively, then refused to loosen.

"Would it bother you more that Seth wants your throne, or that he might be using me to do it?" he asked.

I wanted to correct him that it was Grim's mantle, but who knew how long before he was back? I was, in fact, the acting God of the Dead. And I could be for years to come. There was no guarantee Grim would return at all.

With Grim now reporting to Osiris in the Afterlife, he might find himself reassigned to entirely different duties for all eternity—leaving me stuck here weighing the worth of souls until the end of time.

Before I could think too hard about that or before Aaron could move yet another one of my items to the completely wrong spot, I took the book from his hands. "Is that what he's doing? Using you? How is that possible?"

I needed to know. I had to stop Seth before he started something. My position was too new to believe that Seth wasn't looking for a way to take advantage of the vulnerability of my position.

Aaron's face was oddly void of expression. "It was a hypothetical question."

Oh.

He had been asking me which I cared about more.

Aaron was fishing. He wanted me to say I cared if he were exploited.

Suddenly, I found myself holding the book too tightly.

I carefully reshelved it. Did this mean he wanted me to want him?

Aaron was the one to walk away, not me.

Not that you'd given him a real chance, something in my head whispered with merciless observation. *You told him you could never be together so many times. You might as well have told him to leave town.*

"I'm bothered by all of it," I end up saying noncommittally.

Aaron flicked the highly accurate replica of the Nanchang Star Ferris wheel in China. My patience thinned to a wire.

I stopped the turning wheel by covering his hand with my own.

"Could you stop?"

"Stop what?"

"Stop...*touching* things."

His lips curved up, lined with mischief.

"Oh, I see how it is." I rolled my eyes, finally catching on. "You are driving me mad on purpose."

"Only because it's so easy to rile you up. And you should think of it as a favor. I'm trying to help you loosen up, Timothy."

All my focus narrowed to where my hand was on his. No longer warm when he was human, his flesh was cold but still strong. I should pull away, but I couldn't.

Judging by the way Aaron's pupils expanded outward into dark pools, I wasn't the only one affected by the touch.

Aaron stepped closer, and again I was drowning in the heady mix of his cologne and skin.

"I have another show coming up," Aaron said in a low voice that suddenly hushed the room into a close intimacy I couldn't ignore. "I'd like you to be there."

"Why?" The question came out hoarse, affected.

"You *know* why," he pressed. Aaron's eyes searched mine with fervor as his brows knit in pleading distress.

He wanted me to come for *him*.

Even without speaking, Aaron broadcasted his need. He wasn't over me any more than I was over him. His finger lifted under mine so it parted my knuckles, wedging it there. I fought the urge to shut my eyes. I swallowed hard, throat clicking in the silence. How long had it been since I'd touched anyone much less the man I'd been left haunted by for the last three years? Four years since Vegas, since the warmth of his skin met mine, and now even his vampire's touch burned cold fire up my arm, igniting my every desire and want.

I stepped back abruptly, the very skin on my hand aching and screaming as I separated it from Aaron's.

"You are bonded to Seth," I said, more to remind myself.

One crack in my resolve, and Seth would pry it open wide enough to topple everything I had been entrusted to guard.

Or worse, if Seth caught even a whiff that Aaron mattered to me, he would weaponize him against me in an instant. He'd dangle Aaron as bait, or snap him like kindling, whatever broke me faster.

Aaron's face shuttered. The heat in his gaze vanished all at once, leaving nothing behind.

Ice filled my chest as I was transported to that morning at my place. He wore the very same expression as he told me he was leaving Vegas.

"I should go," he finally muttered.

"Yes," I said. "You should." My heart hurled itself against my ribcage in protest, not wanting to let him go.

Aaron left. The door shut behind him as final as a closed tomb.

On numb legs, I walked to sit behind my desk. My hand closed around the now-cooled coffee cup. I didn't bring it to my lips, just held it.

Everything in me was tearing in two.

Should I have said yes?

Should I stay close to him to better keep tabs on Seth?

Should I stay away from Aaron to make sure Seth never finds out what he is to me?

I stared at the cup in my hand, willing myself to chuck it at the far wall, so that the milk and espresso exploded everywhere in a furious outburst. But no matter how I tried, it remained on the desk, in my hand.

Controlled, secure.

It's what I did. It's who I was.

And suddenly, I hated it.

5

AARON

My chin rose over the pull-up bar, my back and biceps straining with fire.

I should stay away from Timothy. It's for the best.

Lowering my body slowly, my thoughts did a one-eighty as I pulled myself up again.

Now that I've seen him, I can't stay away! I refuse to stay away.

Another pull-up.

No. It would be idiotic to force Timothy into my problems with Seth. I need to get free on my own.

Sweat dripped down my face and torso, audibly hitting the tile floor of my apartment. Or maybe my heightened senses made the droplets seem impossibly loud as they punctuated my violently volleying thoughts.

I'd lodged a pull-up bar in the doorway to my bedroom, a place I could never have imagined living a few years ago. It was one of the high-roller suites in Seth's hotel, and despite the expansive square footage and luxe finishes, it felt more like a gilded cage.

I was on maybe my six hundredth pull-up when I dropped. Still not worn out.

Vampire strength was amazing, but it made it all the harder to work off my restlessness. I walked to the kitchen to get myself a glass of water more out of habit than necessity.

There was one person I'd like to work off this tension with, but Timothy couldn't—no, wouldn't—let himself even entertain doing such a thing.

He'd say it was too dangerous.

He wasn't wrong.

Despite being back in Vegas, I'd stayed away from him for so many reasons. The main reason being the devil I'd struck a bargain with. Seth kept close tabs on me, and if he caught me running to Timothy, I didn't think that would end well.

I was right. Turns out, they had a long history that was anything but chill.

My hesitance was also because I'd also been determined to get out of the mess I'd gotten myself into before I went to Timothy.

The whole plan was to become a vampire to show him I wasn't a weak, breakable, mortal anymore. We were equals now and could be together.

Ha! What an idiot I was.

Timothy looked at me like he always did when I got too close. Like I was a tornado about to touch down on his perfect world and ruin everything.

My insides gnashed with jagged parts of wanting, knowing I'd do anything to make him mine. Even now.

In his office, our hands touching, I'd been on the verge of grabbing him by the throat and pinning him to his perfect little bookshelves. I wanted to ravage him with hot, open mouth kisses until we knocked over all his trinkets and books, and his control snapped like the stupid, brittle twig it was.

But I wasn't free to do so.

I swigged my water, closing my eyes tight, swallowing the frustration.

There was a knock at my door. Frowning, I crossed the apartment to open it and found Miranda standing there. She wore high-waisted black leggings and a snug compression fit, a cropped tank that showed her shoulders and kept her free to move. Bob was sheathed on her back while a lightweight zip hoodie was tied around her waist. Judging by the outfit and the slight sheen of sweat on her body, she'd either just been out at the gym, or monster hunting.

Her eyes flashed with black cat energy. Everything about her screamed "touch me and die." But as the labrador retriever type myself, I didn't much let it bother me.

"Hey," I said, my shoulders dropping a couple of inches.

"Hey," she said with a sharp jerk of her head. "Can I come in?"

"Oh, yeah." I stood back and waved her in.

"Wow." She whistled, her head swiveling to take in all the finishes on my place. "This is a far cry from that shithole place you shared with...what was it? Three roommates?"

"Four," I corrected, as I headed toward the bathroom. "But one of them was always out of town on business so it might as well had been three."

Miranda followed me, her hand casually encircling the hilt of her sword strapped to her hip. I grabbed a fresh towel to mop up my sweat as she nosed around my apartment, opening closet doors and poking into the different rooms. "Your stutter is gone. Is that a vampire thing?"

Straight to the point as always. Miranda never pussyfooted around what she was thinking. A trait I found incredibly reassuring in a friend as well as amusing at times.

"Nah, after I left, I hit my speech therapy with a new zeal. Got it mostly under control." It did still surface, but only when I was under extreme anxiety or exhausted.

She opened my fridge.

Bracing a hand on the kitchen island, I asked knowingly, "Looking for something?"

Miranda closed it again, a water bottle now in hand, shaking it at me. "Just for something to...drink."

I suppressed the need to roll my eyes. That's all she'd find in there. No bags of blood or anything else. While I could still eat human food, I didn't miss it all that much.

She cracked open the top and leaned a hip on the island as well, facing me. She took a long swig then gestured with the bottle at me. "Tell me everything."

A wry chuckle escaped me. "Man, this is a far cry from the girls' nights we used to have with Vivian."

Miranda shrugged, her expression even and unapologetic. "She was always the fun one."

My brows screwed up in offense as I laid a hand on my chest. "I thought that was me."

Her amused smirk faded. "What the actual hell, Aaron?"

My brow raised at the sudden attack.

"You're back in town for months, you're suddenly a—" she gestured up and down my body, "—vampire. What? How? Why? How?"

Watching the normally cool Miranda get tongue-tied would be more amusing if she weren't bringing up everything I wanted to avoid.

"It's a long story." I started to walk by her, but she slammed a hand to my chest, forcing me to look her in the eye.

"I got time," she said in a tone that probably would scare the Cheez Whiz out of anyone else.

I wasn't sure if she developed that voice of command when she served in the army or out of necessity as a single mom.

Even though I was equipped with fangs now, I had to admit to a little Cheez Whiz escaping me when she pulled the authority card.

"You better sit down," I huffed, knowing there was no way out of this.

Situated on the green leather couches that faced each other in my sunken living room, I leaned my forearms on my thighs.

"Two years of trying to forget everything that happened here in Vegas by rafting in Costa Rica, jumping out of planes in Switzerland, and rock climbing in Australia, it was when I was surfing in Japan that I realized I couldn't let it go."

"Let what go?" Miranda asked, eyeing me with suspicion.

Timothy.

Instead, I said, "The lifestyle. The excitement of being near such incredible power and beings. I saw vampires attack, battles between gods. The supernatural turned out to be under our noses all along, and I was on the front lines of it unfolding into the public eye then I just...left it behind."

"And that spiked your adrenaline-seeking behavior?" she asked flatly.

"Probably," I shrugged. "Being mortal is cool, but being immortal? Armed with strength and dexterity like nothing else? I knew I was *meant* for that kind of life. So I decided I'd find a way to become a vampire."

Miranda groaned and pinched the bridge of her nose. I ignored her and kept going.

"It took a long time to find someone who would help me do that. And the only way I could achieve that was by coming back to Las Vegas."

Face still arranged with incredulous doubt, Miranda asked, "And you didn't think to ask your good friend, Vivian? The vampire we know and love?"

I raked my nails through my hair. "By the time I got here, she was gone. So I had to resort to someone else."

"Seth?"

Unable to sit for any longer, I stood and paced the sunken floor. "He found me. He'd heard I'd been asking around. Asking how to get turned. But, as you know, most vampires are too new. So new to their own fangs they don't know how to function, much less turn someone else. So after another failed attempt of trying to find a vampire to turn me in a bar on the outskirts of town, there was this guy. Full of charm and promises, he told me he could help me with my little problem."

A sound resembling the snort of a bulldog escaped Miranda.

"He knew a vampire skilled enough to turn me, but Seth told me if I turned, I would be a danger to others. The vampire who could turn me wouldn't be able to help me control my new...urges." I shook my head, remembering the way Seth swirled the olive in his dry martini. Decked in a fitted striped suit with his slick hair, looking completely out of place in the dive called The Hairy Harbinger, I couldn't tell if he was an angel or the devil.

Turned out it was the latter.

"But Seth said he could help me with that. If I did what he said, he'd make sure I didn't hurt anyone."

This time, Miranda swiped a hand over her face as she groaned.

"Yeah, I know,' I said, flexing my shoulders. "Hindsight is twenty-twenty. Yadda yadda."

What was done was done. There was no use going on about what a gullible dumbass I was. There were only consequences to deal with now.

"He told you to bite him and drink his blood after you turned," she filled in the rest.

I didn't mind skipping over the awkward part of the story where I met up with Seth and the vampire in a room at the Menaggio. Idiot that I was, I didn't even realize that it was Seth's hotel and he was a god.

Yet the whole thing felt eerie, wrong. Still, I had committed to my plan. I knew what I wanted, and I was going to get it. I knew it'd be painful, but I wasn't prepared.

The vampire got a taste of my blood and instantly went berserk.

He tore my throat out with zero control while Seth looked on from his seat, legs crossed, watching like some kind of cuck.

As my neck was ravaged, no ability to scream, my blood gushing out from my jugular, I realized I'd only stupidly served myself up to be a quick meal for a vampire and this was the end.

Then I woke. Naked in silk sheets of a bed I didn't know. Panic spiked through me with hard disorientation, though nothing beat under my chest.

More severe than that was a new, all-consuming thirst that threatened to consume me from the inside out.

Seth swept into the room in an open red paisley robe with black trim that billowed behind him. He only wore a pair of black boxers. For a man who appeared to be in his sixties, he still kept fit and groomed.

Him floating in the room, looking deliberately like a

snack for a hungry vampire, was yet another red flag. But I couldn't process anything other than the thirst, burning me alive from the inside out. He cradled my head to his neck, cooing and encouraging me to drink. He'd take care of me, and in turn, I'd be his golden boy. His lucky charm.

The moment my fangs sank into a god, I was eternally clasped to him as a decorative item.

"Yeah, I did." I shoved my hands in my pockets. "I drank his blood."

Miranda sighed, leaning back on the couch. "I know we dealt with Seth before you were clued in on the supernatural shit, but Aaron, a blood-bond? You knew what that was. Why the hell would you agree to that?"

"I don't know, I didn't think it through." Seth came to me when I was vulnerable, offering everything I wanted.

Even now, I wondered if I'd known Seth was a god at the first, would I have accepted his help? I'd like to think not. But I'd been so desperate to make myself better for Timothy, I might have made all the same dumb mistakes and ended up exactly where I was.

Immortal and bound to the wrong man.

"When Seth said he could help keep me from hurting others, it didn't occur to me that he planned on doing it through a blood-bond where he could control me. I was a starving fledgling. Honestly, I think I would have tried to take a bite out of anyone who'd been nearby." I ran a hand through my hair, the thought souring on my tongue as soon as I said it.

Miranda huffed again then pinched the bridge of her nose. "At least this is something we can easily fix." She stood, her shoulders squared with resolve.

My eyebrows raised of their own accord. "Oh?"

She shot me a look like I was an idiot. "Yes. If you bite

Timothy, a blood-bond with him would break the one you have with Seth."

She was right. Now that she said it, I remembered something in the weird unwritten rule book of vampires that this was a thing.

If I drank the blood of another god, I would be bound to them instead.

As soon as the solution was presented, it dissolved, and I went flat. "That's not an option."

"The hell it isn't," Miranda said with force. "Cut the shit, Aaron. You missed Timothy, and you thought if you became immortal, he'd stop keeping you at arm's length. That the two of you would have a real shot."

My jaw tensed at her no-bullshit callout.

"And sure, you made some insanely stupid moves to do that, but it's romantic as hell. So march your sculpted surfer butt over to that uptight god and tell him you want a taste so you can be his love slave for all eternity."

"Miranda!"

"Aaron!" she yelled back, mimicking my tone.

I collapsed onto the couch, slumped over where I sat. "He doesn't want me."

She crossed her arms. "Bullshit."

My thoughts darkened as I remembered the electric spark sizzling between our hands when they touched in his office.

I was right there.

I basically put myself on a platter for the taking, consequences be damned. But that was the thing. Timothy feared consequences and mess almost more than he feared his desire for me.

"I already went to see him," I informed Miranda.

Her arms dropped as some of the steam she'd been

rolling over me evaporated. "What happened?" she asked, her voice softer now.

I shook my head, unable to forget the invisible wall he threw up between us. "He doesn't want to fight for me." A lump formed in my throat. "Not when it could make waves. Not when it interferes with the balance between gods and politics. I'm not w-worth it."

Dammit. The uncontrollable stutter only tripled the pain crushing my chest.

Miranda sat next to me this time, her shoulder pressed against mine. "He loves you, Aaron," she said quietly. "He's gotten even more uptight and fastidious since you left. Like if he threw himself into work, it would make him forget. But anyone would know he couldn't. Not you."

The lump in my throat doubled, and my nose began to sting. She was trying to help, but what she said only made things hurt more.

"I thought if I became like him, if I became unbreakable, he'd feel safe enough to take the leap." My gaze darkened. "I was wrong."

Miranda licked her lips before biting the lower one, looking off in thought. "I used to be a lot like him. Unwilling to bend the rules, unwilling to bend myself for anyone, afraid I'd break. That everything would fall apart if I let myself feel vulnerable around someone else." Her voice cracked on the last words.

"Then you met a crazy guy in a basement and said fuck it, the sex is too good to care?" I taunted, knowing very well who she bent herself for.

Xander had been a crazy, snarling mess, and every night while she was trying to put him out of his misery with Bob —the god-killing blade — she was also falling for him.

Xander didn't care that she was human, but it became a

non-issue when he was drained of his power and became mortal himself.

She punched my arm. Again, I whined as I touched the spot she hit, pretending it hurt.

"No," she growled before her expression softened. "Well, a little, but a relationship with a god...it's a lot. I didn't take that lightly, and neither does Timothy. He just needs...time."

"Welp," I said, slapping my thighs and standing. "Time is all I have. But right now, I have to head to rehearsal for my next show," I lied even as I led her to the door. "It's going to be a doozy. Can I count on you to be there?" I waggled my brows at her.

"Wouldn't miss your dumbass being suicidal for the world," she said, rolling her eyes before heading out.

As soon as the door closed behind her, dread filled me from the tips of my toes to the top of my head.

I'd been working out at a near manic pace, not only to take the edge off my frustration with Timothy, but to take the edge off another kind of frustration.

A thousand pull-ups and I'd still feel the creep of unrelenting cold stiffen my muscles the way it invaded me now. It felt like dying. Again.

I couldn't ignore the freezing pain spreading through my entire being or the desperate thirst that had me in a chokehold. My eyes squeezed shut tight even as my throat seized with impatient need, my cells turning in on themselves to cannibalize each other.

It took all my willpower to close my hand around that doorknob, twist it, and leave.

The hallway stretched before me with mocking invitation, each step on the burgundy carpet muffled as I trudged the familiar route to the elevators. The distant chime of the bell echoed hollowly. My limbs felt leaden, my movements sluggish against an invisible current as I took the familiar route.

Even in the following few days after Seth bonded me to him, I thought I'd remade my life for me. I thought I'd gotten what I wanted. But I didn't yet realize what I'd done. What I'd allowed to happen.

The crushing, violent need to drink propelled me forward on reluctant feet. I knocked on the double doors to one of the penthouse suites that was a permanent residence and by far the grandest.

With a click, the door opened itself. Seth lounged on the leather sectional, his lean frame framed by an emerald silk robe that lay open.

The blue glow from his phone cast eerie shadows across the sharp planes of his face and glinted off the tortoiseshell reader glasses perched on his aquiline nose—glasses I knew were purely for show, a calculated affectation.

Without even glancing up from whatever had captured his attention, he raised one long, pale finger in my direction, commanding my silence and patience while he continued scrolling with his other hand. The quiet tap-tap-tap of his manicured nail against the screen was the only sound in the cavernous room.

Hands shoved in my pockets, revulsion skated under my skin at what I was here to do. A few more taps, then he finally set the phone down.

"You are up to two million followers from that last video we posted." His grin was victorious, but faced with it, something wilted inside me. The stunts were thrilling. The best hit of life reinforcing adrenaline a guy like me could ask for.

But the followers, the growing adoration and fame...I couldn't care less. But that was what he wanted. I was his new spectacle. My job was to draw a crowd.

"Is my lucky charm thirsty?" Seth asked in a patronizing tone, before straightening and patting the spot on the couch next to him. "Can't have that."

In my original vision, I'd be using one those vampire ethically-sourced blood banks to drink from pouches like they were Capri Sun for the rest of my life.

Instead, there was only one source I could drink from now. Only one blood type my body would accept as sustenance. That's what it meant to be in a blood-bond.

I slunk across the room, feeling like a dog, settling next to him. Seth's arm opened to rest around my shoulders and draw me in. "There's a good boy."

My nose wrinkled before I bit into him. Despite myself, I let out a shaky sigh as Seth's blood welled from the bites, and I sucked his essence down. My cold, frozen body warmed, thawing with the blood I took in.

I drank his raw, electrified power with a stringent aftertaste, but my body responded enthusiastically, my hands clawing at his shoulders and chest as I took more and more.

"There's my golden boy,' Seth patted the back of my head. "What would you do without daddy?"

6

TIMOTHY

Aroar greeted me the moment Miranda and I stepped out onto the Menaggio's rooftop. Wind whipped around us from this high up.

The packed crowds lining every railing gave it the same charged atmosphere as a stadium right before the main event. Spotlights swept across the sky in sharp, feverish strokes.

A thousand humans pressed against the barriers, phones held high, every voice tumbling over the next in a feverish chant of Aaron's name.

My gaze slid to Seth, who had positioned himself on his own elevated viewing platform on the far side of the terrace. A velvet-roped lounge built into the roof's highest corner, perched above the others. Gold-trimmed railings. Plush seating. Personal bartenders. And a faint shimmer of wards woven into the canopy overhead. Yet again, he'd built a throne disguised as VIP comfort, but the intent was obvious.

He was recreating a memory where he was an ancient Greek ruler who would oversee the gladiators slaughtered for his amusement. Anger and fear zipped up my spine, striking my brain with pulses that made it difficult to maintain logic and calm.

As if sensing me, his eyes connected with mine, and that insufferably smug grin widened as he toasted me with his martini glass.

As Miranda said, pure dick pickle move.

"Is that thing permanently attached to this hand?" Miranda asked in disgust.

"I don't like the looks of this," I said as I forced myself to focus on the setup.

Two massive rig towers rose from the roof, each bolted into reinforced steel plates that extended right to the building's edge.

"Neither do I," she said through gritted teeth. "But we need to be here, and you know it."

"Do I?" I countered dryly despite the somersaults my stomach made. I wasn't sure if the internal acrobatics were because of anticipation or anxiety about colliding with Aaron.

With a glance, I caught sight of a gaggle of girls holding signs that said different variations of, "Suck Me Dry." They were already teary-eyed and vibrating with tension at the prospect of seeing the vampire in action.

My predecessor, Grim, never had a need to use social media because I was always the one cleaning things up and scrubbing the internet for anything too damning or revealing about our world. A task which still fell to me even as I judged souls, ran Sinopolis, and managed the affairs of other gods. Which is why it surprised me that I hadn't seen what a large online presence Aaron had before now.

The stunt of riding down the Sinopolis hotel had been a turning point, rocketing Aaron's fame into a stratosphere that continued to compound on itself, as more people shared and discovered the video and then found out what the daredevil looked like under that helmet.

The world fell for Aaron's lopsided smile, blond locks, and recklessness. Then he was revealed to be a vampire, and his fangs only furthered the frenzy. The world's first celebrity vampire.

His face showed up on social media everywhere from the moment I opened my phone and was now plastered all over the billboards along the Strip. The mention of his name repeatedly echoed around me from the guests at Sinopolis.

His follower count broke into the millions and was fast approaching tens of millions. Fan vids and lives were constantly popping up in my feed, making it impossible to ignore the craze he was causing. Everyone on the Strip, across the nation and streaking to other nations, Aaron's death-defying acts had the world in a chokehold.

Can't say I blamed them, but the entire situation made me uneasy.

And not only because there was no longer a single moment I could escape the feeling of being haunted by the man I had spent the most earth-shattering night of my life with.

I shouldn't have come.

Miranda scanned the crowd on high alert. "Look, I know running into Aaron is turning you inside out—"

"He is not turning me inside out," I said too loudly between clenched teeth.

Miranda's dark eyes caught mine.

"I have lived for thousands of years," I explained. "I have met millions of souls. Aaron is just another among them." Even as the words came out, my insides twisted at the lie.

"Okay, regardless of Aaron just being another meaningless person in your many old man years," her tone could not have been more mocking or dry, "Seth is definitely up to something. We need to keep tabs on his bullshit. Even if that includes Aaron—no, *especially* if that includes Aaron."

I blew out an exasperated bit of air. "I don't need this," I muttered. "Not with the Convergence about to take place."

"Oh yeah, Xander told me about that. Wanted me to tell you he was planning on attending. What is it exactly? Some kind of godly peace treaty meeting?"

"It is a rare cosmic alignment that forces all pantheons to reaffirm their oaths not to interfere with mortal governments, human wars, etc."

Miranda blinked.

"It's basically a supernatural Geneva Convention because the stars align."

"Right," she muttered. "And as God of the Dead, it's your job to remind all the other gods you will spank them if they step out of line."

I resisted the urge to pinch the bridge of my nose at the crass assessment. "I suppose you're not exactly...wrong in your summation."

"We'll *both* be there," she said with finality.

I wasn't sure that was the best idea, seeing as Miranda was human and wielded the only blade that could essentially put an immortal out of commission. I wasn't even sure if Xander's presence was a good idea. He was one of the oldest gods, but he'd been human for years. My skin itched at not knowing how to categorize him for such an event.

Miranda's presence, in support of me, could be viewed as a show of power, or potentially an act of aggression. Again, tension gathered between my temples. I was used to juggling a lot, but it felt like if I didn't walk the perfect line, everything would be thrown into chaos. There was too much gray area.

On the far platform, Aaron stepped into view. The crowd exploded into shrieks.

Two women stood in front of us, one holding a sign with Aaron's photo blown up on it. The other livestreamed to her phone.

"He is unreal," one whispered, clutching her chest. "I'd let him wreck me every which way until I died dead."

"No joke. I worship the ground he walks on," the other said breathlessly, angling her camera higher. "No wonder he is blowing up. He is on a whole different level."

A faint hum prickled at the back of my skull. Something about their tone. The hunger in it. The word "worship" hanging in the air with a strange resonance. Plenty of Vegas shows and celebrities garnered attention, but this was something else. Something too focused. Too intense.

Gone were the motorcycle leathers. Tonight, Seth had poured Aaron into a cream and navy stunt suit, all polished buckles, tight seams, and theatrical bravado that didn't belong to Aaron at all. The fabric clung to every line of his body, glossy under the spotlights, a costume meant to market him rather than protect him. Wind whipped his blond hair across his cheekbones, turning him into something mythic. A man I could envision belonging to any time or place in history.

His turquoise eyes locked onto mine. The roar around me dimmed to nothing. It felt like the entire rooftop tilted toward him, and I could fall forward, right into him.

His smile hit me like a punch to the sternum.

Miranda leaned in. "Yeah. Real distant of you."

I tightened my jaw, but I did not look away from him.

"I'm just here to make sure Seth isn't up to anything," I

said to Miranda. "I can't afford to have him undermine me right now."

It had nothing to do with the fact that shivers flooded my body and hot goose pimples covered my flesh, my power rising to the surface with a desire to claim Aaron as mine. To whisk him away from this frenzied crowd where I could peel off that ridiculous outfit until I could trace his bare flesh to my heart's content.

Aaron reached out to grip a metal bar on one of the tower rigs. After throwing a saucy grin to the audience, he pulled himself up and began to climb. With every rung he ascended, my stomach twisted tighter. Then, as he reached the top, spotlights snapped upward to illuminate a wire. A single shining thread stretched between the two metal towers.

Anyone stepping onto that line would have nothing beneath them but a plunge straight past the Menaggio's glimmering facade and down to the Strip below.

Not anyone. Aaron.

He stepped onto the wire, barefoot. He tested the tension with one bounce that sent the line shivering through the air. Then he grinned at the crowd and began to run.

The twisted bits in my stomach plummeted so fast the blood rushed from my head with dizzying force. His silhouette sharpened under the beams, tank top clinging to his torso, hair ruffled by the wind.

I was going to be sick.

Miranda's hand set on my arm. "Aaron has scaled mountains and cliffs. He hooked himself up to all kinds of wires and shit at scary heights when he was human. He dabbled in acrobatics for funsies. If he weren't such a chaotic gremlin, he would have worked in one of the circus shows no doubt. Have some trust."

The wire thrummed under Aaron. Every step was a calculation, a gamble. He planted his feet lightly, arms loose, posture easy. Too easy. He turned, jogged backward, then flipped. The fans detonated. Someone behind me cried from excitement.

"He's crazy," breathed someone nearby.

"He's *gorgeous*."

"He's a motherfucking vampire," another said with a fist pump.

Phones flashed mercilessly and I had to bite down on the sudden violent urge to use my magic and rip them out from the hands of all the onlookers and smash them into a giant ball of inert metal and plastic so they couldn't distract Aaron from this ridiculously dangerous stunt.

My nails dug into my palms so hard they cut deep into the skin. The pain barely took the edge off the tension and fear roiling inside of me.

The humans couldn't see his glow the way I could. To me, he was incandescent. His soul had crystallized into something dense and enduring, light packed tight until it glowed with steady force. Gods were made to feel the warmth of souls, to feed on their potential, and his radiated it in abundance. As if he wasn't tempting enough before.

My heart hammered against my ribs, unnatural for a god who should be steady for all. Yet here I was, pulse racing like I had been thrown into a furnace. I burned with the urge to reach up, to steady him from a distance, to command the wind to behave.

Power pulsated just under my skin.

Take him. Save him. Do something.

A whine came from my side. Assirak had arrived,

sensing my distress. I released my right hand's death grip to pat the reaper dog's head a few times, with false reassurance I was fine.

Halfway across, a gust slammed into him.

The wire snapped upward with a violent shiver. Aaron's foot skidded. His whole body pitched sideways. The crowd screamed. My breath stopped entirely as he slipped, fingers clawing at thin air.

He dropped.

Miranda's reassuring hand on my arm tightened into a death grip.

Aaron reached to grab the wire at the last moment, but his fingers slipped, missing the target.

The world tilted out of focus, and when the blackness in my vision receded, I saw he was still there. Hanging by one hand, legs swinging out over open air. His arm muscles trembled from the sudden load. The wind tore at him. My brain blanked as I lost seconds or maybe minutes to panic, swallowing any rational thought. A feeling so foreign it sent another freezing chill of fear through me.

"Is he going to do something?" Miranda hissed under her breath.

I glanced at Seth in his balcony. He merely watched with interest. But he wasn't watching Aaron, he was watching the crowd as we all had our hearts jammed in our throats. He wasn't going to do a damn thing.

Power tingled in my chest and hands.

"Timothy," Miranda warned.

I didn't have to look to know blue glowing sparks were dancing around me. Thankfully, no one was looking at me. All eyes were rapt on Aaron's fragile, dangling frame.

Even if he was an immortal vampire, he could be hurt.

His head could crack open like a melon. I reminded myself he would heal...eventually, probably.

That somehow didn't make me feel any better.

If he let go, would I react on instinct and throw my magic to catch him? Out myself as a god standing amidst humans? Seth and Grim had their flock of followers and fans but I'd managed to stay on the sidelines and out of the spotlight. Would I do something so crass as flaunt my power among mortals, for Aaron?

I didn't want to find out.

Move, I willed, even as my chest locked so tight it hurt. Please move.

Aaron hauled himself up with a surge of strength that made several humans swoon. He crouched on the wire, breathing hard, then straightened with a shaky laugh that was eaten by the wind, as if nearly dying was part of the show.

Miranda's death claws released, and she patted my arm. "That's our boy. I knew he'd be just fine."

I couldn't answer. My whole body was fire and ice at once.

Because as long as he stood on that wire, I could not look away.

AARON

Rough hands pushed me to the wall with surprising strength. One minute, I'd been toweling sweat from my neck as I left the makeshift stadium through a private service corridor, the next I was being manhandled. Which was impressive because I wasn't technically just a man anymore.

The air still vibrated with cheers and bass from the show.

"Don't you *ever* do that again, do you understand me?" Timothy stepped back, his face so red it reached the tips of his ears. His elegant three-piece suit stood out amidst Menaggio's excess, a single tasteful note amid the cacophony of gilded walls, mirrored panels that screamed money.

He didn't belong in this place. The hotel bent itself around Seth's ego, but Timothy stood there like it all offended him on principle.

I couldn't help the smile from spreading across my face. "You came."

Why was it so hard to stay mad at him?

Maybe because he turned my insides into a carousel ride of dancing animals complete with cheerful music. Or maybe because he was fussy enough for the both of us.

"Yes, I came," he hissed. "I'm here to keep an eye on Seth, to see if he's going to cause me trouble, but no. It's *you*. *You* are the one driving me to the edge of my control."

The edge of his control?

Well, wasn't that interesting?

"I was fine up there," I said casually even as I glanced down at his white-knuckled fists.

It was a lie. My body was still fizzing. The adrenaline laced every nerve ending, the ache in my ribs a living thing. I was seconds away from becoming an exploding flesh balloon on the concrete ground miles and miles below.

Granted, I had extensive healing abilities, but that didn't mean I was in a hurry to test those out. But I wanted to see if Timmy would call my bluff.

"You..." His voice cracked. He inhaled sharply through his nose, nostrils flaring. "I watched you flip—FLIP—on a wire thinner than my finger, hundreds of feet above concrete, with the wind—" He gestured wildly with one hand, mimicking the gust that had nearly killed me. "And you, you reckless fool, I know you are going to do it again."

The next words slipped out before I could catch them. "You could stop me."

He pulled back, just enough to look at me properly. His eyes emitted an eerie glow, casting a warmth from his deep dark irises. "Don't tempt me, Aaron," he whispered.

It hit me then, how terrified he was of losing me. The idea made me dizzy. No one had ever looked at me like that. Like I was precious. Like my fall would have destroyed their whole world.

There was a current of violence contained in his stillness, in the way his chest moved, shallow and quick, in the glare that would have sent mortals to their knees in terror.

I held his gaze, defiant, because I was still flying, still poised on that wire in the sky with the city glittering beneath me. But if Timothy would take the plunge with me, I'd gladly step off from such a great height.

"That's all I want to do," I admitted, as every muscle coiled and tensed with hope.

Reach out for me. Take me. I'm right here. I'm all yours.

He let out a strangled noise, half-laugh, half-snarl, and then stepped away, breaking whatever spell had settled over us. My already cool body iced over.

"This is exactly why I can't form such attachments," he said, voice grave again. "You may be immortal now, but you still seek your own death."

"Good thing you are God of the Dead, then," I shot back before stepping into his personal space, needing to close the distance between us. "This is bullshit, you realize that, right? If you were so afraid of creating connections, why would you be friends with Miranda? You know she'll die one day too. Will you regret spending time with her? Or would you cherish the time you had together?"

"It's not the bloody same," he said, trying to avoid my gaze but not pulling away.

I didn't know getting him this riled up would make him extra...British. Now I wanted to push harder, see what other English-isms I could provoke out of him before he snapped.

"Come on, Thoth," I said, licking my lips. His ancient name delicious in my mouth. "You want me. Why don't you just...take me?' My fingers skimmed over the hairs at the nape of his neck as I pulled his body flush to mine. His clean, masculine scent didn't just wash over me, it saturated me. I breathed him in all the way to my toes and still needed more.

His impossibly dark lashes fluttered, threatening to shut with pleasure. It took everything in me not to throw him on the nearest surface and ravage his mouth. Find the dark depths of him, forcing his strength to meet mine. But I couldn't do that. Timothy had to be the one to break the barrier between us.

Though it would be my fangs sinking in his neck.

A rush of blood exited my brain via the south door.

I gently tilted his head to the side, exposing and lengthening his elegant neck, holding him tighter against me.

"Don't you want me?" It came out a husk as my thirst surged to the forefront, gathering in the tips of my fangs. I gently scratched his jugular with them, my teeth actually ached from holding back.

The god's fingers tightened on my hips at the same time his jaw flexed. Pressed together like this, there was no denying his hardness, the stiffness centered at my own pelvis. I wanted to penetrate, sink into him on so many levels that I was determined he'd end up calling *me* a god while I—

Timothy pushed, letting me go. It felt like I was free-falling backward though I stood stiffly.

When I met his gaze, I found dark lightning flashing in his eyes. "We can't. The rules forbid it." It came out through tight lips.

My own mouth twisted with frustration and petty desire to cover his, kissing him so hard and furious he'd have to soften and give way under me.

"Fuck the rules," I practically spat the words, getting in his face again. "You are a *god*, Timothy. You are the reaper of souls. Everyone must answer to you, which means you can make the rules."

His expression was still flat, unmovable, tinged with a distant sadness. "That means I, above all else, must adhere to the rules. I set the example. If I descend into chaos, then everything else will too. And I simply can't allow that." Rolling his shoulders, he turned to walk out of the room.

I grabbed his bicep, spinning him around. "You need a little chaos in your life," I said before crashing my lips down on his.

The groan he let out could have been interpreted as one of disgust or resistance, but as I claimed his mouth with a hunger that pulsated from the marrow of my bones, he met me with the same fervor.

Short nails clawed down my scalp as I grabbed at him, pulling him fully to me, not willing to let him get away.

We'd kissed before, but that was when I was human.

That alone had haunted me for years. The intense, all-consuming power and passion that replayed every time I lay down to sleep. It was also the first memory I revisited before opening my eyes in the morning.

But *this*, this was two angry, powerful thunderclouds clapping into each other. We struck each other with lightning, electricity rolling through us as we passed the force back and forth, pushing us to a heightened peak.

Timothy's unique taste was addictive, but it soon morphed and layered as our tongues combated for dominance until our kisses tasted like a convergence of both of us.

My head snapped back as he fisted my hair, angling my throat before he attacked it. He unleashed all his frustration on me with scalding hot sucking and biting. My groan was broken and loud. My dick was so hard, I was positive there wasn't any blood left in my brain. The dizzy spell only heightened Timothy's effect on me.

"Fuck," I rasped, bucking my hips, needing more.

Then there was nothing but cold air around me as my ass hit the wall. The contact broke so abruptly my body stayed pitched forward, reaching, while my mind struggled to catch up to the empty space he left behind. Despite no longer needing to breathe, I found myself panting.

Timothy ran a frustrated hand through his hair, cheeks flushed, mouth wet and eyes dark. "No," he barked. I couldn't tell if he was yelling it at me or himself.

Without meeting my eye, he went on. "This cannot happen. The return of Sekhors to the new world is still too new, too tenuous. If I were to rip into another god's blood-bond, it could lead to a brutal war of gods claiming vampires for their own. I would be seen as volatile and weak, and I'd constantly have to defend my position."

I surged to my feet. "This isn't about anyone else, and you know it." Anger seethed from my words. "This is about you, me, and Seth."

It was almost imperceptible but I caught his flinch at my master's name.

His posture softened. "Maybe if...maybe in a couple hundred years...when the political climate has calmed—"

"Or when Grim is back and gives you permission?" I didn't hide the disgust in my voice.

Timothy's gaze flashed at me.

I rolled my eyes. "You think I'm the only one bound? You are so bound to Grim, to this position, to the rules, you are more trapped than I am. The truth is, Timothy..." I stepped closer until our shoulders brushed. "The truth is," I said quieter now, my eyes fixed on some distant point beyond him. My fingers twitched at my sides, fighting the urge to touch him even as I prepared to twist the knife. "You may be a god, but you treat yourself like a mortal. You've chosen fear over power every single time."

Before he could respond, I clipped his shoulder as I passed by him, walking out the door without looking back. Because I didn't want to see the pained look on his face.

Even without looking, I could hear it in the uptick of his heart, of the slight but sharp inhale. I could feel the air rippling around his muscles as they coiled in response to my dig.

The truth hurt, but he needed to hear it. Just like I needed to somehow cut my heart out of his chest and take it back as my own.

8

TIMOTHY

Standing before the mirror, I adjusted the collar of my tailored suit. It shimmered, a star map of constellations embedded directly into the fabric, shifting subtly as I moved. A faint blue glow pulsed at my back, a sigil of my recordkeeping and cosmic order, and unmistakably divine. It was a perfect nod to the celestial theme of the night.

Tonight was the Convergence. Expectation pressed down on me like the ancient stones of the pyramids themselves, looming and heavy. I took a deep breath, reminding myself that tonight was about order, about power.

It was not about snogging with a vampire who had driven me to distraction.

I ran my fingers through my hair, tweaking small pieces, making sure they looked just right. Perhaps it would distract from the deep circles that hung beneath my eyes.

Sleep had eluded me for the last week and a half. It had since I cracked under Aaron's mouth, and my focus had been fracturing like glass underfoot ever since.

Every time I got near the man, I found myself battling a

storm of impulses, selfish desires, and a reckless urge to seize what I couldn't allow myself to have.

My eyes fluttered shut as it rushed back to me in high-def, technicolor. The turquoise of his eyes receding into thin bands around the expanding dark pools of his hungry pupils as he kissed me. The heady scent of him saturating my entire body with a mixture of the ocean, something clean, and deeply sensual.

And his taste…oh gods, his taste. The salty, masculine play of his tongue drove sense from me in tandem with the rough scratch of the scruff on his face. All my blood had evacuated to my cock with painful insistence while my heart had lodged its way up into my throat, beating only for him. Aaron.

A shiver rolled through my body.

"You cold?" A voice pulled me from my trance. I opened my eyes to find Miranda standing at the door.

Her gown was deep indigo, sleek and lethal in its simplicity, the fabric flowing like liquid night. The bejeweled headdress and jewelry glinted with more than glitz. They were captured stars, encased in little jeweled fittings.

I picked it all out for her personally. The gods wouldn't like having a human present, but at least she'd somewhat blend in.

Slits in the skirt showed off her muscular legs, though they were more for function, in case she needed to, as she put it, "kick some ass." To prove the point that she was willing and ready to do so, Bob sat at her hip in an equally ornate scabbard.

"Bob says thank you for the new sheath," Miranda said, catching where my gaze went. "He says, 'Je me sens ravissante.'" *I feel ravishing.*

Miranda's French had improved noticeably over the

years. The Blade of Bane had spent many centuries inert and waiting in France, from the Middle Ages to the Napoleonic era, and from what she'd told me, spoke with the accent.

Bob was also of discerning taste, so that was quite the compliment.

I straightened my shoulders, deliberately calming my body. I needed to be steady, to project control. The weight of my responsibilities pressed down like the centuries I had walked this earth.

"I'm still not sure your presence is a good idea," I said to her.

Before I could answer, the tap-tap-tap of claws striking the marble floor brought my attention down to Assirak. He sat dutifully at my side and looked up at me.

"Alright, if you say so," I answered the reaper.

Miranda's brows quirked.

"Assirak says I need all the backup I can get tonight." I gave Assirak a little scratch behind the ears, more for me than him.

Miranda stared down at what must have looked like empty space underneath my hand. "Smart pooch."

I would have corrected her underestimation of the reaper, but Assirak simply opened his mouth in a happy grin, his tongue lolling out. The reapers seemed to find it a joyful lark to play "dog," as it were.

I extended an arm to Miranda, leading her out of the private suite and to the main room. We were just below the lobby of the hotel, on a private floor.

Dark onyx marble floors and airy, bright ceilings with palms that thrived without access to the sun echoed the design of Sinopolis's decor. At the center of the room was a large silver pool of water, sunken into the floor.

We ascended the few short steps to the edge of the pool. Miranda eyed the water suspiciously. "If my dress gets wet, these gods will get more than an eyeful of what I got underneath."

"Isn't your significant other a water god?" I asked pointedly.

She smacked my arm. "Was. *Was* a water god." Then she murmured as she skeptically examined the pool, "But he does know his way around a pulsating showerhead with what seems like inhuman dexterity."

Assirak let out a small, curious woof at my side.

"Don't ask," I cautioned, then turned back to Miranda. "Trust," I said simply.

I stepped forward.

The water closed over my shoes, cool and electric, climbing my calves, my knees, my waist without getting me wet. For a moment, the world inverted. The ceiling became a lake of light. The chandeliers stretched and elongated, turning into distant stars.

I felt the old pull, the one that existed long before elevators and hallways and discreet entrances for gods who no longer wished to be worshipped openly.

Then gravity corrected itself.

I emerged at the top of the staircase of the ballroom that I had created on a different plane of reality earlier today. A tiny pocket of time and space so the immortals could meet in assured privacy.

I released Miranda's arm now that she was on firm footing.

The Convergence unfurled beneath me in a vast, breathtaking sweep of space and power. The ballroom stretched impossibly long, its ceiling lost to a night sky threaded with slow-moving constellations. Chandeliers floated untethered, massive rings of gold and crystal rotating lazily, each a different planetary body. They all aligned, mimicking the universal order in space.

Thick columns rose in clean, deliberate rows, pale stone etched with hieroglyphs that glowed faintly blue along their grooves. Carved lotus flowers bloomed at the tops of the pillars.

The walls were carved with overlapping symbols of gods, stars, and planetary paths, our stories layered into the stone. Small points of light were set into the walls, mimicking the pattern of stars.

It was ancient design dressed in excess. I allowed a small moment of pride for what I had created. Grim never cared for the frills, but I always felt there was power in ambience, embellishment, and design.

This was undoubtedly my turf, my style, and I intended for every immortal present to feel my power.

As I descended the first few stairs, the guests turned as one.

Every god. Every goddess. Every demigod who had been summoned by the alignment and the oaths it demanded.

Their attire bent reality at the edges. Fabric orbited bodies instead of clinging to them. Veils, like cosmic black holes, absorbed all light that touched them. Jewelry pulsed faintly with living magic. Some bore their true features, eyes reflecting galaxies, skin traced with sigils that shifted when looked at directly. Several had no faces at all.

The sheer density of power in the room pressed against my senses, familiar and heavy, with the weight of memory.

For a heartbeat, I was back in Egypt.

Back when we did not hide. When temples rose in our honor, and prayers were spoken aloud. When humans knelt and believed with a fervor that burned cities to the ground. I remembered the wars that followed. The blood that filled the Nile until it became necessary to retreat into myth and shadow.

That was why this place existed.

Why even now, when the humans believed in us again, we remained restrained.

Miranda fell into step, several paces behind me. I felt more than saw her posture shift smoothly into that of a predator on alert. Despite being a mortal in an elegant gown with a sword at her hip, to the room, she read as a statement. A reminder. I had the favor of a fae blade and its wielder.

Assirak paced at her side, head high, eyes glowing softly. Miranda could not see him, but she adjusted her stride unconsciously to accommodate him anyway.

Good.

I let my power rise.

Not unleashed. Never that. Just enough to be felt. Enough to settle into the marble beneath my feet, into the air, into the chests of every being watching me descend. The murmurs died. The chandeliers slowed their rotation.

The swirling galaxy of light that hovered over my right shoulder pulsated as blue hieroglyphics shed from my skin in faint embers.

If the gods did not respect my authority, if they did not find me worthy to take up Grim's mantle and lead in his absence, this could all break into bloodshed and chaos.

Grim once said a third of the gods didn't give a shit who was in power as long as it didn't interfere with their business, and another third were looking for someone to blame and break for why we did not live by the old ways.

The last third was the most dangerous. These gods and demigods were hungry, foaming at the mouth to break down the barriers to the new ways they wanted to live.

Even now, I could spot the different hungers simmering, barely restrained by certain figures in the crowd. They were waiting for me to slip up. To show any glimpse of a soft underbelly so they could leap and rip it out with their teeth and claws.

I was the thing standing between all the chaos and the modern world. If they didn't buy my authority, if they didn't see me fit...

I made myself hard inside, locking down every stray thought, every fracture that had formed in the last two days.

At least I wouldn't see Aaron here.

The relief was quickly cannibalized by disappointment. Despite everything, Aaron made me feel powerful in a way that had nothing to do with fear or control. He made me feel like myself, and like that was more than enough. Unfortunately, I had to be far more than that today.

I buried thoughts of Aaron for the hundredth time today and continued down the steps.

This was *my* Convergence. My watch. My responsibility.

I reached the floor of the ballroom and stopped.

The silence held.

I lifted my chin and owned it.

"Welcome." My voice didn't boom, yet it broadcasted to everyone present as clearly as if I stood next to them. "Eat, drink, and let us revel in the alignment, not only of the stars, but of our great forces—"

The hairs on the back of my neck all rose at once as my eyes caught on something across the room. My stomach clenched in tandem with my heart.

Not something. Someone.

Behind me, I felt Miranda and Assirak tense. They saw him too. It wasn't my wishful thinking.

Aaron was here.

9

TIMOTHY

Aaron wore a black and gold suit, the jacket left deliberately open to expose his bare chest. The metal of the fashionable collar snapped around his neck caught the light in a way that made it impossible to miss, an elegant signal of ownership disguised as fashion. He looked radiant and vulnerable all at once, long blond hair tousled, turquoise eyes too alive for the role he was forced to play.

Seth stood next to him, a master holding the leash of his pet. His lips spread into a heinous, malevolent knowing grin as he met my eyes.

Cold sweat broke out on my spine as something hot and unpleasant buzzed at the base of my skull.

"Timothy," Miranda murmured.

I snapped to myself, realizing I'd stopped mid-sentence. I cursed my show of weakness. "Our forces," I began again, "bring divinity to the realms and that is worth gathering and celebrating in peace and harmony."

The words barely registered to my own brain as panic swarmed my senses.

Gods raised their glasses as I finished my words.

I did my best to look completely cool and in control, though my every atom vibrated with excitement, anticipation, but mostly, fear.

Having said my welcome, I didn't feel my feet as I traveled across the room.

My sense shouted at me to stop and think, but I couldn't. Not until I stood in front of Seth. I vaguely registered Assirak and Miranda following.

Seth leaned fully into excess. His suit was richly embroidered in gold and crimson, gemstones generously decorating it, the cut immaculate but loud. The effect was deliberate—a peacock display of wealth and indulgence layered over sharp intelligence. He wore confidence like cologne, too strong, too close, and entirely intentional.

My nose wrinkled.

"Seth," I said woodenly.

"Ah, the man of the hour," Seth said loudly, as if he were the ringmaster of a show I was now part of.

My teeth creaked as they clenched. I was careful not to look at Aaron despite every part of me screaming to do just that. To grab him and take him far from here, somewhere secret. Somewhere safe.

"This is a godly affair, Seth. I don't think others will take kindly to you bringing your Sekhor here." My tone was even to my own ears, but I could hear the tightness in it.

Seth snorted into his drink—something deep purple that fogged over the edge of the martini glass, leaving little sighs on the air. "If Grim could bring his bitch to these parties, I see no reason why I can't bring my...companion."

I felt Miranda stiffen as Seth referred to our friend Vivien in such a derogatory way.

I wanted to punch Seth. I wanted to pull my power to me

and blast him across the room. Wield my ribbons of glowing hieroglyphs and wrap them around his mouth and throat and squeeze until—

"Who let the escaped convict into the party?" a new voice interrupted.

Seth's face fell, as displeasure darkened his brows at the newcomer.

"Sorry I'm late," Xander said, leaning over to kiss Miranda on the cheek. Then he wrapped an arm around her waist before full on grinning at Seth.

He'd slicked back his hair, though chunks of his dark locks had already escaped to fall over his piercing cerulean eyes in rebellion. A sheer indigo cape flowed from his shoulders and was embroidered with faint constellations that blurred between tides of deep water and space above. The outfit he wore was enchanted to match Miranda's jewels, trapped stars and galaxies swirling on his suit, just for the evening.

I had to make sure they matched, after all.

"You complain of my immortal consort, but you allow mortals to attend our affair," Seth sneered.

Assirak let out a low growl.

Xander threw his head back and laughed. "Ah, Set, you haven't changed, have you? Still a raging, gaping asshole." Xander's eyes shone with intense challenge, using Seth's old name unabashedly, unafraid.

A glimmer of savage madness sparked from Xander's dark blue depths. Leftover from the many millennia he'd been imprisoned, mad with power and pain. His existence was a danger to everyone and the world until Miranda came along. Xander might be mortal now, but he still thought and moved like a god.

"Since you are so uncomfortable with the company at

this party, would you care to visit your second home?" Miranda fluttered her lashes at Seth.

He reared back ever so slightly. "What?"

Miranda slowly, carefully unsheathed Bob. Immortals nearby stilled or turned toward us as the Blade of Bane glinted under the shimmering cosmos hovering just overhead.

If she'd drawn it any faster, or in any other fashion, it would have signaled a threat. The gods would have lashed out in anger or fear, causing a chain reaction that would have been catastrophic. But this woman knew how to comport herself, even among ancient immortals.

"Oh, what's that, Bob? You want another taste of Set?" she asked out loud, also using his ancient name. Seth's face further twisted and soured at her familiarity with him.

"Oh no, right, I see." She nodded, responding to the blade none of the rest of us could hear before leaning toward Xander. "Bob says Seth tasted like cheap gas station sushi and he'd rather not." She shrugged, sheathing Bob once again. "Oh, well."

A small titter of laughter rippled through the gathered crowd. Seth twisted around with violent promise, silencing the laughter though the smiles of amusement remained.

I can't believe I ever thought Miranda might not be able to handle this party.

Taking advantage of the moment of distraction, I finally allowed myself to look at Aaron. My breath was ripped unceremoniously from my lungs. Even amongst gods and immortals, he was the most gorgeous creature in creation. His blond hair fell in loose waves as always, but the heat emanating from his eyes froze me to the spot.

Without words, they spoke.

I didn't want to come. He made me.

With a slight tilt of my head, I responded silently.

I know.

His cheeks tinged red as he touched the collar around his neck. Again, my anger flashed hot and bright. Aaron was not an animal to be chained up.

I'd rather see him step onto that wire far above the Strip of his own free will, rather than see him locked up and kept like a pet.

Aaron's face hardened into something brittle. The moment passed quickly, but the damage lingered, etched into the set of his mouth and the way he no longer met anyone's eyes. I could see his humiliation and a small part of him actively die as Seth forced him to play his role of blood-bonded slave out in public.

Bile churned its way up my throat, but I fought it back down along with my anger.

I didn't know if Seth was deliberately baiting me with Aaron, but either way, I couldn't let him get to me.

"You don't belong here," Seth hissed at Xander.

At least I wasn't the only one losing the grip on their composure.

"Xander, Miranda!" An excited squeal broke through as Bianca rushed forward. A swirling confection of pink cosmos entered our little group as Bianca openly hugged Xander then Miranda. The blonde oracle goddess with beautiful, delicate features, once known as Hathor, knew exactly what she was doing as she warmly welcomed the mortals.

In her wake followed the lazy stride of a tall Black man with one brown eye and the other glowing bright. Fallon used to be known as Horus, the sky god, and tonight the power he held was unleashed and on display.

Fallon glared at Seth with open disdain as Bianca just

barely held herself back from flinging her arms around me. Instead, she straightened before dropping into a deep curtsy.

"Thoth." She set a hand over her heart. "My gratitude, my loyalty, my power to the one who wields the power of souls. The God of the Dead. *Heri ib.i, her khet.k.*" She finished in the old language.

Above my heart, under your authority.

Fallon continued to stare at Seth coldly, silently letting him know his presence wasn't welcome before dropping into a deep bow before me.

Xander and Miranda barely paused before doing the same. It created a ripple effect. I twisted to watch as the rest of the gods all around began to dip in the same deference, the old words murmured in respect.

Turning back, I found Aaron gazing at me with that lopsided smile that made my heart skip a few beats before tripping all over itself. He looked at me like he was not only in awe, but like he was proud. Something I never thought I needed from another being, but I drank it up like water from an oasis.

Aaron slowly began to bow.

"No," Seth ground out. Aaron's body stopped cold, going stiff. His eyes widened a moment in either surprise, pain, or both.

My fingers twitched, energy flowing to their tips in reaction to Seth bending Aaron to his will. Hieroglyphs swarmed angrily around me.

Seth was the only one standing in the ballroom apart from me, and his eyes darted about, noting how the rest had bowed in deference. Aaron was caught half bent over, but his eyes flashed hatefully at Seth.

I tilted my head at Seth in a silent challenge. With the

entire ballroom showing me respect and obedience, he had a choice to make.

Many in the room who bowed may not actually share the respect Bianca had exemplified, but they stayed in line to keep in favor. Would Seth do the same? Or openly challenge me?

With great reluctance, Seth finally bent over, a grimace plastered on his face. Aaron gasped as he was suddenly released from Seth's invisible hold so he could complete his own bow.

Realizing this moment was one to take advantage of, I gathered my power to my fingertips, flooding them before throwing out my arms. Ribbons of glowing hieroglyphs sprayed out from my hands, extending to gently tap each god or goddess on the shoulder in acknowledgement before they swirled upward. After receiving my touch, everyone rose to watch the churning swirl of my magic weave between the floating planets in a web that showered sparks.

Closing my eyes, I considered pulling the power of souls I reaped to further show my power. I decided against it, instead allowing my power to fade and rest.

I opened my eyes, and after a beat of stillness, the entire ballroom resumed motion and the dull roar of conversation.

Seth simply curled his lip at me before turning and walking away, presumably to get another drink and lick his wounded pride.

Aaron stared at me with such open wonder and lust that heat curled in my stomach before dropping lower.

He jerked, his chain yanked by Seth to come along. The sensual heat I felt twisted and sharpened to the point of a knife, piercing my heart as I watched Aaron disappear into the throng.

A hand on my shoulder drew my attention to Fallon.

"Well done," he said with a nod of approval.

"*Very* well done," Xander added with a smirk.

Bianca simply clasped her hands together with a sweet, delighted smile.

"Well, is this a party or not?" Miranda asked sharply. "Where are the snacks? Where is the dancing?"

"Right away, my love," Xander said, kissing the back of her hand before guiding her through the crowd toward the tiered displays of crystallized fruits and carved meats.

"You're doing so well," Bianca said quietly with a pleased smile before it faltered. "But the night is far from over." Her irises disappeared behind a white film as if she were seeing a vision. "Too many doubt. They do not think you are powerful enough." The white faded away. Her eyes returned to normal as her brows knitted in concern.

"You need to find your power," she said, gently touching my lapel, right over my heart.

I nodded, my throat suddenly thick.

As I parted ways with them, Fallon leading Bianca by the arm, I knew she was right. But it was hard to logically think how I'd find my power when all I wanted to do was turn over everything I was to the collared, indentured man bonded to my nemesis.

But I had to put Aaron aside and do what I came here to do.

Show the others I was in every respect, the God of the Dead.

10

AARON

Seth was angry. Even as he smiled and schmoozed the room, I could feel it coursing in my veins, a pulsating poison through our blood-bond. Occasionally, I'd catch an angry mutter about Bianca or humans before he once again donned his charming persona. And here I was, stuck at his side. His dog.

My instructions were to just stand by and look pretty. He said I made him look good, though I had a suspicion Seth had an ulterior motive in showing me off. Not that he'd tell me.

While I had no problem showing up as a wingman or plus one to help a friend at the occasional wedding or night out, this was nothing like that. I was unmistakably Seth's pet. The same as the reaper dog I now saw at Timothy's side most days. Though I had a sneaking suspicion that the reaper dog was allowed far more dignity and agency than I was.

As if on cue, the creature trotted by, and I couldn't help but look at him with jealous longing, which really hit home how messed up my life had become.

The dog paused its canter to swing its head up and meet my gaze. I was struck by the strong sense this creature possessed a great deal of intelligence, calm, and maturity.

It tilted its head ever so slightly, eyes glowing a faint gold. A strong sense of reassurance from the reaper flowed into me. He saw me and acknowledged my predicament. He twisted his head, and I followed his gaze to see Timothy across the room. He was engaged in conversation with a small group of gods, his hands tucked behind his back. He needed to stop that. If he was so hot to exude power, he needed to stand with his arms at his sides. Hands behind his back made it look as if he was hiding something or waiting to serve someone else.

Huh. And here I thought I never benefited from that communications course at the community college I dropped out of.

Timothy's eyes slid to the side, meeting mine for just a moment. His intensity, his longing barreled into me—a physical force. Every muscle in my body tensed as a wash of tingles swept through me. I was suddenly panting, though I didn't even need to breathe.

It had been like this since the first time I met him at Sinopolis. I'd burned through one city after another, chasing bigger drops and sharper adrenaline, until the desert felt like the next logical mistake.

I was in the middle of receiving my orientation to work at Perkatory from an older woman named Angela when Timothy approached. Nose stuck in his tablet, fingers flying, I could practically see calculations churning off his brain in wisps of steam.

"Sir," Angela had greeted the man with unexpected enthusiasm for someone who slung cappuccinos to make ends meet. "You caught me training the new guy."

"Excellent, Angela, we would be lost without you," he'd said, digits still tapping away at whatever he was working on while somehow giving the impression he was completely present and engaged with the woman he was speaking to.

Then he looked up, and my heart dropped. It fell right out through my ass and careened toward the molten core of the earth.

I never really had a type. I met interesting men of all kinds who I enjoyed getting to know and spending time with, but suddenly I knew I would only ever want this. Someone like *him*. A kind of man who had intense dark eyes that broadcasted an arresting intelligence. I could tell in an instant I would never be bored with him.

From the tight line of his lips, I'd spend most my days coaxing them into yielding and softening under mine. And his hands. I can't say I'd ever been turned on by a man's cuticles, but there was something so precise and appealing about them. My fingers itched to run through his charcoal black hair, perfectly set, the texture sharp and intentional.

Then he smiled at me. My heart rocketed back up from the core of the earth reentering my body with extreme violence before blasting my ribcage into one of those deep-fried blooming onions dishes. I was cooked.

In the present, Timothy's attention returned to who he was speaking to, and the moment was over.

"Interesting." The word slid into my ear—a poisonous snake.

Seth stood next to me, looking on at Timothy, stirring the dark blue of his cocktail with a toothpick adorned in a garnish that wasn't a food item I was familiar with.

Something in my chest pinched tight, with sudden fear. "What?"

Seth then grinned at me with all the menace and

promise of a cartoon villain, and my stomach churned in sick anticipation.

"Oh, nothing," he said without meaning it, "I just continue to be impressed by your usefulness."

The urge to chew my arm off to escape the trap he'd set on me was strong. But there was no way out of this. My heart squeezed so violently with every glimpse I'd catch of Timothy across the room, I could have sworn it almost started beating again.

The lights dimmed in the ballroom as a hush fell. Everyone's attention turned to Timothy as he strode through the crowd and toward a dais.

The blood in my veins came to a halt.

No longer in a suit, he wore ancient Egyptian garb.

Gold and lapis crossed his chest in deliberate lines, the ceremonial collar broad on his shoulders. White linen wrapped his waist in sharp folds, secured with a belt etched in hieroglyphs older than language.

Bands of gold circled his arms and wrists, snug against warm skin. In his hand, he held a staff capped in gold.

I wiped drool from my mouth. Timothy in a suit was devastating, but this was a god. His biceps flexed under the straps, his abdomen carved marble under the chandeliers. And then the air shimmered.

His head shifted.

One blink and the man was gone, replaced by the sleek, inhuman elegance of an ibis: long, curved beak, feathers edged in moonlight, the divine intellect of Thoth staring out from an avian gaze. A god's body with a beast's head, regal and unreal, power radiating in quiet waves.

It should have been unsettling. Instead, my stomach tightened and heat rushed through me. He wasn't just beautiful. He was magnificent.

He stood at the center of the ballroom, the point every-thing else orbited. Gods in silks and armor filled the space, their power thickening the air. Ceremonial music throbbed low.

My heart cracked as I took in his perfect stillness. Whether faced or feathered, he radiated responsibility, composure, and centuries of watching the world turn. His shoulders carried the room. His eyes, human or ibis, never rested. Duty wrapped him like a second skin.

And it only made him more breathtaking.

This wasn't the Timothy who ordered lattes or flinched when I stood too close. This was Thoth in full glory, holding the world together through sheer refusal to let it come apart.

Standing there among the gods, something painful settled in my chest. This was the version everyone else got. The one who belonged to the universe.

And I had touched the man underneath.

Timothy reached out and pulled down a floating star system from the ceiling, letting it hover in front of him, shimmering with celestial beauty.

I watched, captivated, as he manipulated the galaxies with his long, dexterous fingers. His voice filled the ball-room, steady and commanding. "Just as the planets circle their stars in balanced harmony, we immortals must recognize the interconnected rhythms that bind us. Though we may keep our distance, we are still drawn together by a divine rhythm essential to our existence."

His words resonated deeply, and my body felt weightless as I followed his movements, the smooth track of the stars and planets in front of him. It looked like a hologram, but I couldn't assume anything. Maybe Timothy truly held galaxies between his hands.

"In my duty as the God of the Dead, I reap souls and judge their fates. Each soul I encounter releases energy that strengthens us, allowing our pantheon to maintain its power and influence across realms. The more souls I judge, the greater the energy available to all, creating a symbiotic relationship that sustains our immortality."

I hung on every word, marveling at how he embodied both authority and compassion, proving that even in Grim's absence, he was more than capable of maintaining balance.

As Timothy's passion grew, his voice brimmed with confidence. "I have the wisdom and strength necessary to navigate our complex existence. I am the keeper of records and the judge of souls—"

"Kiss me," Seth murmured but quietly enough that no one would hear him but me. I lifted an eyebrow at him in both confusion and disgust. I didn't speak but my answer was plainly written on my face. *No.*

Seth's forehead smoothed. "I wasn't asking."

Power gripped me from within, jolting me straight as he compelled me through our bond.

I woodenly closed the distance between us as his nonverbal commands echoed in whispers in my mind. It choreographed my hands to lay on his shoulders as I leaned in to inhale his overpowering aftershave that made my nose wrinkle and sting.

"In my duty as God of the Dead." Timothy was still speaking. "I maintain the balance and order of the passing of souls. I—"

Timothy's words faltered the same moment my lips found the column of Seth's neck. My lips parted so my tongue could swipe and press against Seth's skin in open-mouth kisses.

Timothy cleared his throat.

Seth sighed contentedly even as he continued to watch Timothy, as if nothing were going on. I tilted my head while obeying Seth's command so I could see the stage.

Timothy's eyes flicked towards us, his composure fracturing for a fleeting moment. The galaxies between his fingers wobbled as if the cosmos itself felt his distraction. I could see the jealousy creeping in, like a poisonous vine choking his focus.

Timothy's knuckles whitened around the staff, and his voice, once steady, now wavered.

And then his control slipped.

For the briefest instant, the god-mask faltered.

His ibis head flickered and the smooth planes of his human face flashed through, jarringly mortal and exposed before the divine form reasserted itself. Another pulse hit him, his image stuttering between god and man, the shift so fast most mortals would miss it, but every god in the room would not.

He swallowed hard, forcing the transformation down, but the effort shook him.

"I...I ensure the smooth transition of souls," Timothy continued, but the conviction had drained from his voice. His eyes darted back to us, locked onto the spectacle Seth was forcing me to create. I could feel Seth's satisfaction pulsing through our bond, a sickening sense of victory that made my stomach churn.

Seth's hand found its way to my waist, a possessive grip that made my skin crawl. I wanted to wrench away, to scream that this wasn't what I wanted, but my body was no longer mine to control. I was a puppet, and Seth pulled the strings with a smug smile.

Timothy's words slowed, his speech becoming labored.

His ibis form wavered along the edges, feathers

dissolving as Timothy tried to hold himself together. His head snapped into human shape with a rough, uneven tear of magic that made several gods exclaim. The strain showed in the tight lines of his jaw and the tremor in his hand on the staff. He had not meant to shift at all. And now everyone knew it.

The room's atmosphere curdled, the gods murmuring to one another behind raised glasses and hidden smiles. I could hear the whispers, the doubts that Timothy was truly fit to fill Grim's shoes.

"He seems distracted by Set," a voice muttered from the crowd. "Like Set is making him nervous."

"I thought he was supposed to be the smart, eloquent one," another chimed in with a low snicker.

"This is what happens when Grim leaves a scribe to do a ruler's work," someone near the dais said, not bothering to lower their voice.

I finally broke away from Seth's neck, gasping as my eyes locked onto Timothy, who stood frozen. His face, usually composed, was marred by distress, the galaxies he conjured flickering as doubt seeped into the air.

No longer content to whisper, the gods returned to their own conversations. As if Timothy wasn't there.

Several drifted toward Seth with the oily glide of predators recognizing a new alpha.

"So, Seth, how did you get a blood-bonded Sekhor? And where can I get one, or twenty?" The laugh that followed was disgusting.

"Oh, Seth, how about we revisit that idea of yours with fight rings under our casinos? We could pit the humans against each other. Bring back the days of gladiators. Wasn't that a delicious time?"

A goddess with gold eyes tapped her nails on her glass.

"Or we open a club that siphons life from patrons. Offer a lucky streak at the blackjack tables that slowly drains their years. They would line up for it."

Laughter rippled through the cluster. Not quiet or subtle. The sound rolled across the ballroom.

Timothy stood in the center of it, the star system drooping at his fingertips. Every idea dropped by the gods was a direct violation of the order he had spent millennia maintaining. Every one of them was a line they were no longer afraid to cross.

The gods' words echoed in my ears, each word a further chipping away of his authority. I could see the realization hit him—this was not the powerful display he'd intended.

"What are you saying?" The goddess Bianca entered the ring. Her beautiful features were creased with distress. "We must abide Thoth and the rules set for us to maintain peace and balance."

A goddess in red waved her hand toward the dais. "If he cannot hold the room, he cannot hold the power Grim left him. Someone else should take the scales."

The god with the shining eye pulled Bianca away though she looked reluctant to go.

Timothy's shoulders slumped, and I understood then: Seth had won this little battle. He'd used me to do it.

The god of chaos had orchestrated my humiliation, and Timothy lost the faith of the gods that he could confidently rule.

Laughter rose, sharp and pointed, and the sound carved Timothy out of the room.

His authority cracked. The gods measured him, he failed, and now they were deciding what lines they could cross.

For the first time, I fully understood why Timothy kept

his distance. Why he pushed me away. Why he feared what we could cost each other.

If he fell, mortals suffered.

If he faltered, gods like Seth would take over. I looked about me, surrounded by gods with terrible intentions and zero fucks left to give.

My insides caved in on themselves as I regretted ever coming back to Vegas.

11

TIMOTHY

I wasn't going to abandon my self-pity to answer the door for whoever knocked, but they persisted until I was forced to tear myself from the couch and face the intruder.

I winced at the harsh light from the hallway as it cut into my darkened suite with unapologetic violence. The Ink Spots played mournfully from the record player, adding to the absolutely pathetic visage I'm sure I made.

Aaron stood there, back in a regular tee shirt and shorts, his throat freed from that insidious collar. Even as I faced him at my lowest, I couldn't help but feel the sharp pinch under my ribcage as I met his brilliant blue eyes, the hues of the Caribbean Sea.

Aaron's gaze traveled from my bare feet up my legs, over my boxers and silk robe, past the deep lines beneath my bloodshot eyes and my distressed hair, before settling on the sweating tumbler in my hand. It still had a few swallows left of my Gin Rickey.

His mouth tightened at the same time the edges of his eyes did. In disapproval? In surprise? In pity?

My senses were swimming in too much gin to tell.

"May I come in?" he asked, carefully. As if I were potentially volatile, as if I might slam the door in his face.

Ha. Like I could ever.

I stepped back, sweeping a hand in defeated invitation. Aaron already permanently lodged himself somewhere in my chest, he might as well enter my apartment.

He closed the door behind him, returning the moody darkness to my environment, to the hole I crawled in and didn't relish leaving anytime soon.

My mouth turned dry as I remembered the last time Aaron was here. Flashes of his sun-tanned flesh flipped through my mind with startling clarity considering how much I'd had to drink.

An ached developed along my palms as they remembered traversing over the contours of his muscles. A tingling need began in my lips, having nothing to do with the gin and everything to do with the knowledge of how Aaron expertly used his tongue and teeth between mine. I brushed my cheek with my knuckles to quiet its craving for the rasp of Aaron's stubble grazing it.

I tipped back the rest of my ice-cold drink, downing it in one go.

Aaron pushed his hands into the pockets of his shorts before removing them a moment later, as if he didn't quite know what to do with them.

"I'm sorry," Aaron said abruptly. "I-I didn't mean too—I didn't want—"

I held up a hand, silencing him.

I studied him, torn between greedily taking him in and trying to decipher the puzzle he presented. How he was able to have such complete and utter power over me.

I opened my mouth, shut it with a shake of my head, and

returned to the open globe bar for another Gin Rickey. My sixth, or maybe my seventh. I didn't know and didn't care.

As I poured a generous amount of gin over ice, I finally said, "You don't owe me any explanation. You are entitled to do as you wish." Even as I said the words, the poisonous sting in my heart flared all over again like it did on that stage, seeing Aaron lave his tongue over Seth's jugular.

The spoon clinked as I stirred with care, afraid the memory of Seth's eyes closing in sensual satisfaction under Aaron's touch would shatter the glass.

"That wasn't me," Aaron insisted in a firm voice.

Turning around, I waved a hand, making my way back to the couch. "It doesn't matter."

"The f-f-fuck it doesn't," Aaron said, his stutter resurfacing as something hot burned in his eyes.

I blinked.

"You are bound to Seth," I tried to speak as coolly as possible. "It's the natural order of things. And I let your situation get the best of me. The gods' faith in me has been severely shaken, and it's my own stupid fault." I said the last words into my glass as I sipped.

Aaron ripped my glass away and threw it across the room, where it shattered against the wall, leaving my hand hanging empty in the air.

"I didn't want that. I don't w-w-want *him*." As his stutter worsened, the veins in Aaron's throat throbbed with obvious aggravation.

"I became a v-v-vampire to be with you." Aaron's nostrils flared. "I knew you would never be with me as long as I was f-fragile, human. So I became this." He opened his arms. "For you."

Despite his outburst, my voice was quiet and calm. "Are you saying this is my fault?"

He shook his head. "No, but I'm saying we're better together. Stronger together. And I'm sick and tired of you denying it."

I was on my feet in front of him so fast a cool breeze swept across my naked chest from my robe billowing around me.

Only the brief flutter of Aaron's lashes indicated his surprise as I stood there in his face, fists clenched, near shaking, chest heaving as if I'd run halfway around the earth.

I grabbed his face and crashed my lips to his with all the unrestrained fury I felt. I let myself take everything I always wanted.

Aaron tensed for only a moment before he pushed back, opening his mouth, clacking his teeth against mine with desperation. The rake of his scruff across my face fanned the hot flames of need in me to an incendiary level that threatened to melt down the whole hotel.

I hungrily devoured his clean masculine taste. It melted and morphed on my tongue to something deeper and darker.

He grabbed my hair in one hand while gripping my bare hip in the other so tight I knew his vampire strength would leave a bruise. Good. I wanted it. I wanted him. I wanted him to mark me inside and out, to leave an Aaron-sized imprint on my body and essence so I'd never feel the absence of him ever fucking again.

The very thought tore a snarl out of me as I ripped his shirt over his head and backed him into a wall, attacking his neck, sucking and biting, making him mine.

Aaron's moans volleyed between pleasure and pain.

Once upon a time I would have held back. But not anymore. Not with the crash of desire overwhelming my senses. Not now that he was a vampire and could handle all I had to give.

It had been too damn long. The control that bent to near breaking around Aaron had finally snapped, and I couldn't even say it was the gin.

Blood rushed to my cock and the room tilted. My knees buckled beneath me, and I sank to the floor, steadying myself with one hand against the wall as the edges of my vision darkened.

Power and energy pulsed out of me in ribbons of glowing blue hieroglyphs that I sent to the button on Aaron's shorts. He sucked in a breath, stomach muscles clenching.

The fastenings released and my power tugged them down over Aaron's perfect ass, revealing his thick, hard, straining dick already glistening with precum. Unable to help myself I took the head of him into my mouth.

"Ahh," Aaron let out a cry as he gripped my hair and the wall behind him to keep steady.

Gods, the taste of him.

The feel of his thickness, the soft yet strong veins that pulsed against my tongue were beyond any divinity or magic I'd experienced.

Even with his skin cooled from his vampirism, he still somehow tasted like sunshine on a beach. My curiosity about something that had been plaguing me since I saw him again as a vampire finally won out.

Replacing my mouth with my hands, I pulled back to look up at him.

"How are you able to remain so bronzed without access to the sun?"

Aaron looked at me, dazed. I waited for my question to

penetrate, and as I did, I could have sworn he was on the verge of blushing.

"Errr, one of the benefits of staying at the Menaggio is there is no short supply of spray tan booths."

"You've got to be kidding me." I couldn't help but laugh, as he smiled sheepishly.

Needing more, I took him back into my mouth until I nearly gagged when he reached the back of my throat.

"T-T-Timothy." His voice cracked and stuttered. I absolutely relished his inability to keep coherent. I wanted him a stuttering, mumbling, groaning mess. It was only fair I splintered him into pieces the way he'd done to me.

My hand joined at the root of him as I sucked like my life depended on it.

If I couldn't keep to the rules I'd so rigidly kept to for all time, I was going to break them all.

Aaron's nails dug into my scalp as he tried to push away. I resisted but eventually he asserted his supernatural strength to rip me off.

A string of my saliva ran from the thick tip of his dick to my lips, and I was a transformed god looking up at him from my knees. One who gave into every dark, twisted whim. One who gave zero fucks about others, or keeping order.

I wasn't the god of wisdom. I wasn't the scribe who spent his time diligently recording the events of life in service to others from fear, from duty. I was the one making waves, shaking life until it tremored all around us.

Aaron's eyes widened, pupils dilating until they nearly swallowed his irises. His jaw slackened, and his breath caught audibly in his throat as he stared down at me—at what I had become in that moment.

The way I'd abandoned everything I'd stood for...for him. And freedom surged through me.

Then his gaze darkened and vampire teeth flashed. Aaron yanked me to my feet, ripping off my robe as he pushed me back onto the couch. My boxers tore away under his hands and he dove down, taking the entirety of me into his mouth in one lunge.

I bucked up into the sweet wet sanctuary of his mouth with a shout. Oh gods, I had dreamed of this. I had replayed the memories every night, my entire being always begging to get back to here, and it was finally happening.

Aaron gripped my hips, lifting them off the couch and they instantly pistoned, needing more, unable to stop from seeking the wet pressure pulsating and encompassing me.

When he released me from his mouth, seeking to claim my lips again, our bodies slid against each other, both covered in perspiration.

"I love you," Aaron said, all fierceness and teeth even as he kissed me, gripping my hair like he'd never let me go.

I didn't want him to.

Dueling for dominance with his tongue for a moment, I broke long enough to say, "I love you too. I've always loved you."

12

AARON

Timothy's lips curled into mine with a smile, and I smiled back before I could stop myself, holding him to me and savoring the way his abs tightened and dragged over my stomach. I laid a hand over his chest, thumb brushing over his nipples. He sucked in a sharp breath, the sound low and wrecked, and it went straight through me.

We rolled together, all heat and mouths and hands, until I was back where I wanted to be, buried deep in his throat while my hand worked him with a steady, ruthless rhythm. When he lifted his head, my cock slid free with a wet drag. I met his gaze. What used to be warm brown had gone dark.

"Please," he rasped.

The word hit me harder than anything ever had.

I didn't hesitate. I hauled him up, carried him down the hall while his mouth worked my neck, his teeth scraping just enough to make my vision spark. The second I set him on the bed, he lifted his legs, hips tipping up in open invitation.

Timothy held out a hand and the nightstand opened, a

bottle of lube rising and rushing to his trembling hand. I was already wet from his mouth, but I greedily took it from him, slicking where I wanted to go. Timothy gasped as the cool liquid hit his exposed backside. I took my time, making sure he was as teased as he was slippery before dropping the bottle on the ground.

I swallowed, slow and deliberate, pressing the head of my cock where he wanted me most.

When I pushed past the tight ring of muscle, he shouted. The sound tore out of him, raw and unguarded.

"That's it," I growled, jaw tight. "Take it. Take all of me."

He stretched around me, breath breaking, hands gripping the sheets, needing something solid to hold onto. I sank in until I was fully seated inside him, and he gasped in pleasure and pain.

"Gods," he breathed.

Sweat dripped down my spine, my arms shaking as I fought the instinct to drive into him hard and fast. Holding back took everything I had.

"There's been no one else," he said suddenly, voice rough.

I stilled.

He wasn't asking. He wasn't bargaining. He needed me to hear it.

"Not for me either," I said, and meant it.

His throat worked. "But Seth—"

"No." The word ripped out of me. "Tonight he...he compelled me. Made me come to you."

His hands clenched in the sheets. His eyes burned.

He leaned up, forehead resting against mine, and for a second we just breathed each other in. Or I did. He shook beneath me, like he was holding back something violent and incandescent.

I kissed him to stop us both from thinking.

I pulled out almost all the way, then pushed in slow and shallow. He gasped into my mouth, every nerve lighting up. I did it again. And again. Each thrust landed exactly where he needed it, where he couldn't hide from it.

My pace turned punishing. Controlled. Relentless.

The last time we'd done this, it had wrecked us both.

Even when I'd been mortal, I'd turned his world upside down. But now my strength matched his. My body could take him. Hold him. Keep him.

I didn't stand a chance, and neither did he.

He wrapped his hand around himself, breath breaking as he stroked in frantic, uneven pulls. Sweat slid off my hair, splashing his stomach, and the sight of it nearly undid me.

"That's it," I murmured, voice gentler than my hips. "Come for me."

He cried out, head dropping as he spilled hard across his stomach. I leaned down and licked him clean without breaking rhythm, watching his face twist as he felt it.

The look he gave me burned itself into my brain.

"Lick it up," he said hoarsely. "Taste me when you come."

I drove into him harder, the command snapping something loose. My hands clawed at his chest, the bed, anything I could grab as I came inside him with a broken shout.

My body shook. His clenched tight around me.

Then he said it.

"Bite me."

My eyes flew open.

The word echoed louder than my pulse, louder than the rules, louder than Seth, louder than anything except the truth sitting heavy in my chest.

I wanted him. All of him.

And I didn't care what it cost.

"Do it," Timothy said, his hand guiding my head to his neck. My fangs elongated being this near to him. So tempting, so delicious. Mere millimeters separated me from everything I wanted. Timothy. His blood, his body. A bond he couldn't run from anymore. Maybe I should've felt shitty about trapping him into a bond but all I felt was bone deep anticipation and pleasure as I sank my teeth into his neck.

Warm, heavenly blood sizzling with power spilled into my mouth, and all my cool left me. I grabbed him to bring him closer with a pathetic moan as I drank him up. His blood was perfect, as delicious, as layered as the man himself. I sucked and lapped at him, giving myself over to him.

Take me, and I'll take you.

Except, nothing happened. Other than I was drinking the most heavenly blood to exist. I pulled away to look up at Timothy and noticed the tension in his eyes and mouth. Something was wrong.

Then a force smacked me bodily away from Timothy and I was back on the opposite side of the room. Pain detonated in my mouth, starting at my fangs and spreading outward in vicious pulses, pressure building until my vision whited out and I staggered. I cried out in pain as I doubled over. His blood churned in my stomach like some kind of acidic poison.

"Aaron?" Timothy asked, approaching me before I threw out a hand. Then I ran into the bathroom and expelled all of Timothy from my body.

13

TIMOTHY

Aaron clutched the edge of the toilet. A sheen of sweat covered his face as he sat against the tub, eyes closed, exhausted.

I remained standing, eyes fixed on him, every instinct screaming to intervene while discipline locked me in place.

"We didn't bond," I said, confirming the obvious. My words were far away from my own ears.

"What did I do wrong?" he asked, clenching his eyes tight as if bracing himself.

I swallowed hard. The puncture wounds on my neck throbbed with pain and need that radiated throughout my entire body, but it couldn't erase the terrible realization.

"Nothing." It came out a harsh whisper. "It's not...it's not you."

His turquoise depths opened to reveal a much darker, deeper ocean. "Then it's..."

I turned away and reached for a book left out on a table and put it on the shelf. To ground myself. To keep from going to him. To stop myself from touching him, from screaming, from demanding he bite me again.

"Timothy, don't leave me."

His words slammed into me, and I turned as he stood on shaky knees.

"Talk to me, Timothy. What the fuck is happening?"

I clasped my hands to keep from grabbing him and helping him stand.

"I couldn't do it."

His brows quirked in confusion. "You stopped me somehow? Why?"

I shook my head. *Get the words out, man.* "It's been a long time since I've known of something like this to happen," I forced myself to speak, though it hurt. The words hurt before they even hit the air. "But there was an account of a god attempting to forcibly take a Sekhor from their master. He forced the vampire to drink his blood, but the goddess the vampire was bonded to was far stronger. The god could not break their bond, she kept her hold over her slave."

Aaron shook his head, as if not comprehending. "You didn't force me to do anything. And you are the God of the Dead. You are the most powerful of them all."

His words only drove the pain of the truth deeper into me like hot spikes.

"Apparently not." I met his eyes.

Seth was stronger than me.

Despite having power over all the souls of the undead, that dick pickle had more power than me.

The shame, the disgust was almost too much to bear.

"Timothy, we can fix this—"

"No!" My voice boomed through the room. "I can't have you, Aaron. We can't be together. I'm not strong enough. We failed. Seth owns you, and I can't save you. We tried to break the rules, and it didn't work."

That crack at my center split wide open.

We were stuck like this. Even when I broke down and abandoned all the rules meant to keep things in order, I was forced to face how inadequate I was. To face that I didn't really possess a lick of control under the circumstances.

"I never wanted you to save me," he said, his voice low and hoarse. "I wanted you to love me."

My lungs burned with the need for oxygen, but I couldn't force them to work until the door slammed shut behind him, the sound cracking through me like a gunshot.

I walked to my office on wooden legs—an automatic motion.

What to do in crisis?

Work. Organize. Research.

My eyes landed on the neatly organized pens, tablet set just so, various decorative items of Egypt to remind me who I was.

The numbness inside me made way to a heat that started low and insistent before it flamed through me with a fury I couldn't control. With a powerful sweep of my hand, everything on my desk went flying. Objects cracked and slammed into the bookcase.

More décor and books shuddered and rocked under the onslaught. The sounds of things breaking gave me a millisecond of relief, so I chased it. I punched into the bookcase, kicked at the desk until wood flipped and crunched under my fury. I followed the outburst until I was standing in the middle of my ruined office, chest heaving and knuckles bleeding.

You're not strong enough.

You are just playing like you have control.

Seth's deplorable words slithered around between my ears, biting relentlessly at my gray matter.

Yet I couldn't deny that the one time I broke the rules, it didn't even matter.

Suddenly, the rules I relied on to keep order in the world became a noose that tightened around my neck. Falling to my knees, I dropped my head into my hands and screamed in frustration.

~

Steam wafted off the mug of coffee Miranda set in front of me.

"I'm sorry to bother you so early," I said without looking up from the twisting vapors. My words were flat, emotionless, though I was anything but.

"Don't be ridiculous." Even as she spoke gently, there was a challenging bite in her tone. "This is exactly where you come. Now take a sip and tell me what happened."

I wrapped my stiff fingers around the warm mug. It seemed to take forever to bring it to my mouth, but when I did, I finally looked up at my friend. She was awash in warm pink from the predawn light filling her kitchen. The usually hard-edged woman looked softer sitting across from me at the small breakfast table, legs crossed in her robe, braids wrapped up in a silk scarf with a coffee of her own.

Unlike the sleek, streamlined decor of Sinopolis, her house was cozy, lived-in, and well off the Strip. Driving away from the hotel, it got a little easier to breathe with each mile I put between me and it. My responsibilities, my failures.

I forced myself to drink the hot, dark liquid. Miranda made a strong cup, which I appreciated.

"I tried to take him." The words came out softly.

"Aaron?"

I nodded numbly. "I told him to bite me, but it didn't work." Despite the sickly churn of the coffee in my stomach, I took another long pull from the mug.

She hesitated. "It didn't work?"

I shook my head. "It has been recorded that in very rare cases, a Sekhor cannot transfer from one god to another."

Transfer. I had to resist the need to snort at my own description of the situation. What an elegant, inadequate word for what I tried to do. I tried to rip Aaron from Seth and claim him as my own.

Her brow knitted. "Why not?"

I licked my lips, not relishing saying it out loud again. When I did, it came through clenched teeth. "Because Seth is stronger than me. I am incapable of taking what's his."

It galled. It galled so terribly that I wanted to smash this mug against the wall and scream like an angry, wounded animal. But I didn't. I wouldn't make such a scene in my friend's home.

Instead, I brought the coffee to my lips once again, hoping to drown my feelings.

Miranda leaned back in her chair as if needing a moment to absorb the news. She crossed her legs in the opposite direction as she looked out the glass door that led to the backyard where Assirak and her dog were running and leaping about, playing with each other.

Not that she could see Assirak still, but he had insisted on coming. He'd waited outside the shower, sensing my distress, and the moment Miranda texted back that I could come over—even this early—he was already at my side.

The lump that had formed in my throat watching Aaron reject my blood hadn't gone away, but it ever so slightly shrunk. For a moment, I could pretend I wasn't a god, that Miranda wasn't an immortal-slaying warrior. We were just two regular friends drinking coffee and talking about our problems.

"Do you think he's really more powerful than you?"

"If this happened, it must be true."

She shook her head. "Timothy, you are your own worst enemy. Now I've only been walking among the immortals for five years, but from what I've seen, you've been trying to *think* your way to power. Call me crazy, but I don't think that's how you can rule over other powerful ancient gods."

"I'm the god of wisdom, of writing, recordkeeping, and science. *Of course*, I think my way through problems." I couldn't help the testiness creeping into my tone. I was getting sick of being told my way was not the way to do things.

"I'm not saying you shouldn't depend on your strengths," Miranda countered, unfazed by my attitude. "I'm saying, you've been relying on the rules instead of yourself."

"What do you mean?"

"You and I both know that Seth is undermining you. That he's up to something we haven't pinned down yet," she said quietly. The danger of the situation more apparent, it felt imminent, though neither of us could figure out what he was doing. "Why haven't you done something to stop him? To put him in his place?"

"Aside from the fact he's more powerful than me?" I snorted into my coffee with disdain.

"Aside from that," she affirmed.

"Because there isn't sufficient evidence yet and I have to abide by the proper process before I can—"

"You give your power away to the rules," she leaned in as she interrupted, "to a system that is made up. You have the power to remake them, whether you're God of the Dead or not.

"You sound like the other gods. That's what I'm trying to prevent. From any of these upstarts taking this world and reshaping it to what they want."

"Why would you doing that be a bad thing? No, seriously, don't look at me like that. You have been technically ruling this world alongside Grim for a long time. You're not some jackass trying to throw everything over for their convenience."

"That's what I tried to do with Aaron," I mumbled.

"That's different."

"How?" I demanded.

"You love him," she said. "And he loves you. You didn't tell him to bite you so you could take a slave, so you could serve your own ego. You want him because he makes you a better man, a better god. And I know he feels the same and would trust his life and his will to you. Stop apologizing for it and bending to the rules and semantics that don't apply here."

"What are you saying?"

"I'm saying you've been holding yourself back. You are in charge of your life, of this world, but you keep giving your power away to the rules, to Seth. You need to stop. Trust yourself, Timothy. The rest of us already do."

Before I could even gather my wits to process, Jamal shuffled into the kitchen, rubbing his eyes.

"Morning, Mom," he greeted, his voice still rough with sleep.

"Morning, baby," Miranda said, accepting a kiss from her son. He was so tall that he had to bend over to reach her cheek.

"Oh, hey, Timothy," he greeted with a sleepy smile before crossing the kitchen to grab a cereal box and a bowl. His pajama pants rose several inches above his ankles, showing he likely went through yet another growth spurt recently.

Despite seeing him regularly, I was always surprised by how fast he grew up. At fifteen, Jamal had more character to him than most men I encountered. Not to mention a kind of precocious intelligence.

"Whoa," Xander said, his eyes widening when he entered the kitchen next, catching sight of me. He wore a pair of boxers and a wrinkled Hawaiian shirt left open. His hair was a wild mess that stuck up in all directions.

My brow furrowed. "What?"

"You look like shit."

"Language," both Miranda and Jamal chided in chorus.

"Thank you, Xander," I said flatly.

Xander's mouth curved in a smile as he opened the sliding door to the yard. Assirak and their dog bounded in, smelling of morning dew and fresh-cut grass. Both went directly to Jamal, where he avidly petted them.

Miranda snorted.

"Don't be jealous," Xander said as he poured a cup of coffee.

"Yeah, Mom," Jamal said, "I may be able to see the reapers, but you have Bob."

Assirak's eyes closed as he leaned harder into the head scratching Jamal gave him.

At a young age, Jamal had died for a short while. When Grim pulled him back from the Afterlife, he was able to see reapers, and I suspected he'd been graced with a few other extra senses.

Miranda huffed this time. Xander leaned down to kiss her cheek too. "Who's my fussy morning grump?"

She playfully thwacked him on the chest while my

thoughts turned to what Miranda had said, properly chewing on her words.

Did I trust the rules and protocols more than myself?

"So," Xander said as he leaned against the counter, casually sipping his coffee. "Are we going to kick Seth's ass yet, or what?"

14

TIMOTHY

Fremont Street hit me like a physical force. Neon glared overhead in streaks of blue and red while bodies pressed shoulder to shoulder, the crowd electric with anticipation. Flames burst from the parkour rig in the center of the street, throwing heat across the pavement and turning the course into a living hazard. The perfect arena for a reckless god to flaunt his power.

And I had come here to stop him.

I moved through the crowd with purpose, Miranda and Assirak at my heels. After this morning, after admitting I had been hiding behind rules instead of using the authority I actually possessed, something sharp and decisive had settled inside me. I was done watching Seth endanger Aaron. I was done pretending restraint equaled wisdom. Today, I would act.

In the center of it all, an elaborate parkour course was set up, adorned with flaming hoops and fiery obstacles that flickered dangerously, creating an enticing blend of danger and allure.

Before I could reach Seth on his makeshift throne, the

crowd erupted as Aaron stepped onto the starting platform. Fire washed over him in waves of reflected gold and copper. His sleek black helmet and outfit clung to him as he rolled his shoulders and crouched to launch.

Even from this far away I could see the vampiric glow of Aaron's hardened soul.

"W-what is he doing?" Panic closed off my throat.

"Vampires don't do fire," Miranda confirmed, tension in her voice matching my fears.

The audience roared as he launched into action, effortlessly leaping over flames and vaulting through hoops, each move more daring than the last.

"We have to stop this," I said, pushing my way through the crowd to get to Seth.

His bodyguard crossed his arms in front of me. Power flashed so hot off my eyes I saw the blue cast on his face.

"Move," I said firmly.

"It's alright, Jocko," Seth's voice filtered down.

If Seth hadn't called off his dog, I would have gone through him.

"What do you think you are doing?" I demanded. Panic, a wild pack of rabbits jumped every which way in my chest, making it hard to think.

He lifted an eyebrow, looking down at his martini before meeting my gaze again. "Having a drink?" He said the words as if I were a stupid child.

I grabbed the glass and smashed it on the ground. Seth only passively looked down at the ruined drink.

"Vampires can't withstand fire. You are going to get him killed."

The energy peaked as Aaron approached another challenge. He jumped on a motorcycle then revved it up, preparing to jump a massive pit of raging fire. My throat closed off even tighter.

"And what does that matter?" Seth said with a shrug, waving his hand and materializing another martini from thin air. "He's mine to use as I see fit."

"You son of a bitch," Miranda growled from behind me.

"He's not some expendable toy for your amusement."

Seth sat up this time, baring his teeth at me. "That's *exactly* what he is, and there isn't anything you can do about it." His eyes glowed with bright, hot hate and satisfaction.

Power whipped about in my chest with a fury I'd never felt before. It snapped inside, begging to be let out, to be unleashed on the smug bastard who thought he had me.

A collective scream pierced the air. I twisted around.

"Oh my God," Miranda breathed even as I struggled to absorb what I saw.

Aaron miscalculated his jump, and the audience knew what would happen.

Panic clawed at my insides, hot and suffocating, as I struggled to break through the veil of inaction.

Aaron's body hung suspended against the night sky for one perfect, terrible second. Then physics reclaimed him. He dropped short. Flames engulfed him in a violent burst as he hit the pit.

"No," I whispered, the word barely making it past my lips.

"Aaron!" Miranda cried out, while every part of me froze in silent screaming horror.

Each second stretched painfully as I fought to absorb the horror unfolding before me. The overwhelming urge to move, to save him, collided with the crushing weight of helplessness. I couldn't blink, couldn't turn away as the flames consumed Aaron, a guttural scream caught in my throat.

No vampire could have survived that burst of fire.

Aaron turned to ash before my eyes, and with him so did every part of me that mattered.

Screams wailed as the flames erupted higher, illuminating the night with a menacing glow, consuming the figure within moments.

He was gone. Aaron. He was dead.

I couldn't think. I couldn't feel.

It was my nightmare, and I couldn't register what just happened.

I'd stayed away to keep him safe.

No, I stayed away so it wouldn't hurt. So I could survive this very thing.

Then it was like a bomb detonated in my chest, ripping me open. I slowly looked down, expecting to see a blown-out cavity where my ribcage was.

After all that, I lost him anyway and the devastation...

The roar of the crowd faded until I heard nothing. My vision blurred, the world around me dimming as every part of my internal being ripped itself apart in screaming agony.

It didn't matter. It never mattered. No matter how I tried to keep myself safe, how I tried to stay away, I was still here, and Aaron wasn't, and it hurt as if we'd spent millennia together. But we didn't. I wasted time. I wasted all my moments with him.

I hurt him to keep him away to prevent this and it never mattered.

A new rush of murmurs rolled over the crowd, an incoherent buzzing to my dulled senses. Only when Miranda grabbed my arm did I bring myself to look up again.

Just when it seemed the horror could not deepen, a helmeted figure emerged from the smoke.

Confusion twisted a knife to my internal chaos.

Was it his soul walking from the fire, ready to cross the afterlife? No, when vampire souls crystallize, they cannot move on from their vessel. My eyes couldn't comprehend what they were seeing. I forced my lids to blink to clear my vision, but he was still there.

"It's him, oh my God, he survived."

"Can vampires do that? I thought they couldn't survive fire?"

They can't. There was absolutely no way Aaron survived that conflagration...

The helmet came off with a cascade of sun-bleached waves, revealing Aaron's familiar face to the astonished crowd.

The cheers erupted in wild, unrestrained screams as Aaron waved.

"What?" Miranda said next to me. "How?"

My mind calculated faster than the speed of light, putting tiny details together. Something was different about Aaron's glow when he started the stunt, the way his face was now etched with tension and paled despite his smile as he let the crowd witness his death-defying feat.

People reached out, desperate for just a touch, a brush of Aaron's hand, and he obliged as he walked by, headed toward us on Seth's dais.

I was caught in the icy grip of truth. It hadn't been him doing those stunts. Whoever had caught fire like that was gone.

15

AARON

Seth was waiting for me in the Menaggio's VIP club, along with Timothy and Miranda. I recognized a number of the gods from the Convergence in attendance, hanging about with cocktails. Ones I didn't care to see again.

I couldn't bring myself to even greet my friends before tearing into Seth.

"I t-told you—I told you even a vampire couldn't pull that stunt off." Anger and grief shook every fiber in my being. "Tony didn't have to die if you just listened to me!" I was yelling now. Maybe not a wise call since the god I was currently shouting down controlled my very will, but I couldn't hold back.

"Tony?" Miranda asked, looking between us.

"A vampire stunt double," Timothy supplied before I could. His voice was flat, but with one look I knew he was anything but. It was in his eyes. He'd been shaken to his core thinking it had been me that went up in flames.

I swallowed down the near irresistible urge to go to him, to hold him and remind him I was here. I was whole.

"And what did I tell you?" Seth said, unbothered to the point of boredom. "The crowd loved it. You just skyrocketed to the most followers on social media ever in the history of, well, ever." He chuckled as he lifted his phone to show me the staggering numbers.

I didn't care, and I didn't want to be some idol.

The only reason I ever fell in love with stunts and extreme sports was because of how it made me feel. Because of the rush, the endorphins, the pride in achieving something that pushed my mind and body past its limits.

That was never what this was about for Seth. I felt so used and stupid for letting myself be used.

Looking at the numbers himself, Seth said, "The video is still flooding with views to see a vampire defy death. You're more than just a daredevil, a handsome rogue. I just made you a god." He was always a smug bastard, but there was a new edge to it.

"B-but a vamp—" I stopped, jaw tightening. "A vampire didn't d-defy death." Part of me was trapped in the moment. The other part was counting how long I'd been stuck.

I fought the stutter, but my emotions were white hot, and my P's and D's were caught up in an unforgivable web my brain and my tongue couldn't bypass. The harder I fought it, the worse it got.

Seth rolled his eyes. "Well, this is just too pathetic. And *exactly* why I don't let you open your mouth to do crowd work. We certainly can't have everyone knowing what a dunce you actually are."

The words slammed into my chest, striking parts of me I'd thought had healed years ago. My insides curled and blackened, transporting me to that dark place I'd visited on so many occasions after that surfboard slammed into my throat, leaving neurological damage in its wake.

Pathetic.

Weak.

Frustration built inside me, a red-hot backlog I couldn't purge because the words refused to come. My eyes burned with unshed tears as my tongue failed to shape what I wanted to say. My voice caught behind a locked throat. My thoughts looped uselessly, tangling tighter every second as I failed to get them out.

They ricocheted through my head, clogging everything further until my face twitched and my speech broke into short, fractured bursts. My hands curled into fists so tight my fingers went numb.

"What the hell did you just say?" a dangerously quiet voice asked.

Through my blurred, watery vision, I caught Timothy's face. His eyes darkened, and he was deathly still. For the first time, even as I continued to tic and stutter in painful humiliation, it registered that Timothy was the God of the Dead. And right now, he looked like impending death.

Seth didn't even pause to consider the danger he might be in, articulating louder. "I said he's—"

Power surged out of Timothy in a violent expansion, muscle and glowing blue energy flaring at once. Ribbons of hieroglyphs shuddered into existence around his body, vibrating with barely contained force, like live, wicked snakes ready to tear into the closest person nearby.

Timothy's hand closed around the other god's throat. Feet left the floor. Seth's face flushed deep red as Timothy lifted him effortlessly, grip tightening with lethal intent.

Timothy's eyes rounded as they turned to black marbles —inhuman, the same way they had when he took his ibis form.

"Never. Call. Him. Pathetic." The words ground out of Timothy, heavy with dark, dangerous magic.

It was then I realized what this was really all about.

Seth *meant* for Tony to die, and he meant for Timothy to see it. He wanted Timothy to believe it was me and watch him lose control. With a quick glance around, I saw all the attending gods were watching the outburst too.

I was an idiot.

I tried to call Timothy's name, to calm him down, but my throat locked again, breath stalling mid-chest. From the outside, I knew I must have looked like I was ticing, my jaw jerking as I fought for the word.

Even as he clawed at Timothy's grip around his throat and his face turned red, then purple, Seth never stopped grinning.

Miranda unsheathed Bob, her teeth a feral grimace. She was waiting for Timothy to give her the go-ahead to end Seth. He'd be trapped in the blade again, for eternity this time.

"I can call him whatever I want," Seth spat out so violently, his spittle hit Timothy on the nose.

"No," Timothy said, his voice resonating through the room, not caring who heard, who saw him in his power. "You will not insult him or hurt him in any manner whatsoever. He may be blood-bonded to you, but you answer to me, the God of the Dead and keeper of souls."

Warmth settled deep in my chest when he came to my defense, but a warning still prickled at the edges of my senses. Like we were standing on the edge of something big. Something terrible.

A slam of glowing green power forced Timothy back several feet, almost throwing him off-balance, but he regained his ground.

From under his lashes, Timothy sent a cutting glare at Seth.

Power sizzled in the air, crackling against the small hairs on my body and raising goose pimples across my skin.

Seth simply brushed off his suit. "Unfortunately, little *Timmy*," he said with bored impertinence, "That doesn't work for me anymore."

"I gave you a chance, Seth—" Timothy started, but before he could finish, Seth raised a hand in my direction.

A scream of agony ripped out of some animalistic place inside me. My feet lifted off the ground, dangling uselessly as white-hot pain engulfed me so fast, I thought I'd been set on fire. The fibers of my entire body vibrated with violent convulsions. My muscles clenched so tight I bit my tongue, hard. It built and built until I was sure my eyes would squeeze out of my head and pop like grapes.

Wind rushed up through me, tightening into a violent spiral that pulled at me from every direction.

The smell of ozone stung the inside of my nose along with something bright like lemon and sunshine, while the copper tang of my own blood filled my mouth.

Energy ripped through me and out of me—a violent siphon that roared so loudly I couldn't tell whether Timothy screamed my name or if I imagined it.

I was blind to everything except bright, hot swirling energy.

With a crack, my cheek hit the floor. I'd been released from whatever force hit me. I was on the ground, dazed, still feeling woozy from the intensity. It all happened so fast...

"Aaron. Aaron, are you okay?" a panicked voice asked as I was helped up.

Timothy held me to him as he patted my face and extremities, looking for injury. I buried my nose into his shoulder, inhaling his calming scent. "I-I'm okay." Whatever happened, it unlocked my brain from the prison it had been stuck in. Still, I leaned heavily against Timothy to borrow strength.

I lifted my head in time to see Miranda charge Seth. He snapped his fingers, and she froze to the spot, her face etched with a deadly grimace.

Seth glowed with warm, bright light. It pulsed, filling the space. Gasps of surprise rippled through the room.

"What did you do?" Timothy rasped, even as he held me up.

"Your dog here was right to be suspicious. I have been a very naughty boy." The curve of his lips made him look like the devil.

"While I personally haven't been taking worship from souls of the living, he has," Seth pointed at me. "The more attention, the more followers, the more fans and views and attention from pathetic humans so starved for novelty, the supernatural, and honestly a good spectacle, he has been accruing a great deal of power without knowing it. A receptacle for power, an inert battery that can't use its own energy. But now that I've pulled that power through our blood-bond," His words turned sonorous, the reverberations hammering deep into my bones. "I am the most powerful god. I do not have to answer to you anymore. You will answer to me."

With a snap of Seth's fingers, Timothy fell to his knees before him.

A rumble had Timothy looking around at the gods witnessing his subjugation.

Dammit.

It wasn't just about humiliation. Seth was making an example to prove to the rest of the gods that he was stronger than Timothy and it was working based on their expressions.

Even on shaky legs, I launched myself at Seth with a feral snarl that tore my throat raw. My fangs extended to their full, aching length, saliva flooding my mouth with the primal anticipation of ripping into his flesh. Every cell in my body screamed for his blood—not just to drink it, but to violently wrench it from his veins until he collapsed like a desiccated husk at my feet.

I was going to drain him dry until he didn't have an ounce of strength left to hurt anyone.

I got within arm's reach of Seth when my body ground to a halt, muscles seizing as though I'd slammed into an invisible wall.

"Ah, my little boy toy," he purred. Then he snapped his fingers, and my arms and legs jerked around in an unnatural dance as something from above yanked my limbs.

Turning my gaze up even as I danced around, I caught sight of strings from a crosspiece of wood pulling taut in every direction from where they were connected to my wrists and knees.

My stomach flipped then flipped again in dawning horror as I took in that I was now wearing a flamboyant red, white, and black jesters outfit complete with puff sleeves and pants. The faint strains of a circus tune floated in the air.

Humiliation burned its way through my throat as I couldn't stop or control my movements. The watching gods tittered with humor and delight.

"You dick pickle, I'm going to slice you from nose to naval," Miranda snarled from where she was stuck.

Blue hieroglyphs shot out from Timothy with an audible whoosh, right at Seth.

I blinked and suddenly I was across the room, facing down the snapping whips of power headed right at me. Despite their cool coloring, a searing heat bloomed with every millimeter they swallowed between us.

I shut my eyes, bracing for impact, for whatever searing deadly power was about to slice through me.

"You see?" Seth purred again. "I have all the power now."

I opened my eyes to find the pulsating tendrils of power near shivering with barely restrained energy as they stopped a mere inch in front of my face.

Looking past them, I met Timothy's gaze. His face was screwed up with anger, pain, and what I could best guess to be regret.

"And I plan to keep it," Seth snapped his fingers once more, and we disappeared from the room.

16

TIMOTHY

"I'm going to kill him," Miranda said for the tenth time, pacing rather violently along the concrete flooring of Echo's large underground warehouse.

Countless screens flickered across the far wall, cycling through anime, surveillance footage, and dossiers only Osiris understood, while Echo typed furiously at the desk beneath them.

It had only been a couple hours since Seth disappeared with Aaron, and the moment it happened I realized how horribly I'd failed.

My brethren still lingered in the room, watching me with cruel amusement or pitying gazes. I'd lost everything in their eyes. My power, my sway, my status.

I was no longer the one they'd answered to. I'd fallen right into Seth's plan for public humiliation to strip me of my power.

I'd failed to keep the mantle of God of the Dead sacred.

I failed to keep Seth in check.

Worst of all, I failed to keep Aaron safe. He'd blipped out

of existence along with Seth to only heaven knew where, but certainly out of my reach.

Rage and despair warred for dominance inside me, until my teeth cracked from clenching my jaw and my heart threatened to burst from my chest.

Everything had gotten out of hand. Which is why I'd resorted to coming to Echo, a fae so grouchy she was practically crusty with it.

Regardless of her dislike of the gods, the heavy-set Samoan woman hobbled on her cane over to her spot where she spent her days hacking to fulfill my request. If she could pull this off, I'd ply her with an endless supply of computer parts and floral muumuus.

Across from the tech-heavy part of the warehouse, a cozy living space was set up in the middle complete with a large area rug over the concrete floors, a floral couch set, and Victorian lamps that cut the cold computer lights with their warm glow.

Jamal and Xander sat with Echo's husband, Ryuki. With Seth out there, I couldn't leave them vulnerable. I wouldn't put it past Seth to target them. Afterall, Miranda did possess the only blade that could hurt him.

While I could do absolutely nothing. I'd proven to be powerless and an utter disappointment. I couldn't take Aaron from Seth when I had the chance. I couldn't see what was coming even when my sole attention had been on Aaron, the centerpiece to his plans. And even with the utmost power at my disposal, I had bound my hands up in rules that were meant to empower me.

I swallowed back the bitter feelings, acid burning my throat as I forced them down. Self-pity would only waste precious seconds while Seth had Aaron. I may have failed, but I had a plan.

"I don't understand, don't you wield all the souls of the dead? Doesn't that make you the most powerful of all the gods?" Aioki asked as she spun around in a desk chair until I was dizzy watching her.

The teenage Asian girl was dressed in her usual school uniform. Sharp-cut black bangs were offset by the playful pigtails that were bound by fluffy purple ties. Despite being hundreds of years old, she did in fact still attend a local high school. Though I couldn't say if she went because she was bored or simply wanted to be social.

From the way Jamal stole glances at her, I'd say Miranda's young son was rather smitten. If I wasn't mistaken, they were in a lot of the same classes at Neon Valley High School.

I swallowed the bitter pill before speaking. "I do, but souls of the living are far more powerful than those of the dead. An ocean of dead souls cannot combat a couple thousand of the living."

And Seth now wielded millions of living souls. I fought against the pulling drag of hopelessness that threatened to pull me under again. "It's why we forbid gods to take worshippers anymore. I should have known. I should have figured out Seth's plan, but I was distracted."

Distracted by Aaron. By trying to resist him and what I felt. If I hadn't hesitated, hadn't held myself back, I would have claimed him and prevented Seth from using him so poorly, and from getting away with such treachery.

"Well, also," Xander leaned back on the floral couch, a cup of green tea in hand, "No one has ever thought to use a blood-bonded Sekhor like a separate bank to hold all that power until they cashed it out from them like a damn ATM machine. It's...it's godsdamn diabolical is what it is."

Xander uncrossed his legs to reach over and hold out his cup to Ryuki for a refill. Unlike Echo's permanently sour disposition, her husband was always ready with a kind smile and pot of green tea to welcome any visitors.

"Seth should never have escaped the Blade of Bane," Echo huffed from where she sat, her fingers not even pausing as they flew across the keyboard.

Miranda and Xander flinched almost imperceptibly while Aoiki turned away abruptly, but not before I caught the raw pain in her expression.

They were the reason Seth, along with a countless number of other monsters and gods had escaped Bob's prison back onto our plane. It had been to save Xander, and they were still dealing with the consequences. Miranda's full-time job was hunting down the beings that needed to be reimprisoned.

Seth just made the list.

But we couldn't touch him now.

"So if Seth is all powerful, what exactly are we doing here?" Jamal asked, tactfully directing the conversation away from his mom and adopted dad.

"We need to get a message to Grim," I answered, arms crossed so tightly over my chest that my knuckles blanched white against the charcoal of my suit. Each heartbeat sent a fresh wave of dread through me. I needed to know where Aaron was. Now.

"I thought they went into the Afterlife to work on some secret mission for Osiris?" Jamal said, petting the small white rabbit with black rings around its eyes.

Darth Vader had all but melted into a puddle on Jamal's lap. Lulu, a brown rabbit the size of a medium dog with ears longer than Darth Vader's body, lay at Jamal's feet, splayed out on the floor with his legs sticking out behind him, only a few crumbs of Cool Ranch Doritos sprinkling the carpet around him.

Echo may be prickly, but the way to her hard heart was always through treats for her familiars. The fae rabbits had a very specific palette for bananas and junk food.

Assirak lay next to Lulu and they occasionally traded affectionate licks.

"I spoke with Hraf-Hraf," I said, "the ferryman in the Afterlife, and Grim and Vivian have traversed so far into the Underworld that they may have entered an alternate universe at Osiris's behest."

Miranda's brows raised at Echo. "Can you do that? Find people in another universe?"

Echo simply threw her a scowl with a gruff harrumph.

The things Echo could do as a fae being would probably blow Miranda's mind. After learning about the centuries-old woman operating out of the basement of the unassuming industrial building, I'd long since done my research on the magical little family.

"My love could hack her way into the stars above or hell below," Ryuki said in a thick Japanese accent with a heavy dose of pride and admiration.

Echo didn't turn around, but her face softened with a small smile.

"But if you got Grim to come back, what is he going to do that you can't?" Jamal asked.

A sickly lurch sloshed in my stomach. I combatted it by tightening my tie until it practically choked me. "The other gods respect him, fear him. He could rally more support. In greater numbers we just might be able to take on Seth, and cut him down with Bob, recapturing him."

"Bob says he'd rather chew dirt," Miranda chimed in, "but as long as we give him a nice cleaning and sharpening afterward, he's game to take that scumbag down."

"I'll give him a cleaning," Echo muttered.

Miranda's face flitted through some emotions as she undoubtedly heard what Bob had to say about that. Based on her face, his words were very loud and or very impassioned.

"Uh, it might be better if we use Timothy's blacksmith again," Miranda posited.

"I'm not ham-handed," Echo yelled, directly looking at the blade. "You are a sissy and could use some sharpening from someone who knows how."

"Why don't you do what Grim does?" Jamal asked the question again.

The room stilled, a heavy weight around my failures.

"I'm not strong enough," I said. The words hung in the air, a bitter confession I never wanted to voice. Sharp pangs jabbed at my heart, each one reminding me of my failures, of the moments I should have acted but didn't.

The memory of Aaron purging my blood replayed in my mind, a haunting reminder of rejection that cut deeper than any blade. How could I admit to anyone that I felt powerless? They all expected more from me—more strength, more control. I was the God of the Dead, yet here I was, crumbling under the weight of my inadequacies.

"Well, how can you get strong enough?" Jamal asked, his face tense with concentration and thought. He was like me in how he calculated and problem-solved, unable to let go of a problem once he sunk his mind into it.

"Take souls of the living," Aoiki said from where she absently spun for the eighty-sixth time. "Fight fire with fire."

"I can't break the rules," I said, a little harsher than I meant to. Aoiki paused her incessant spinning, and I felt the eyes of everyone on me, even the rabbit familiars.

"Timothy," Miranda said, compassion in her tone.

I broke them for Aaron, and it didn't matter. I was

willing to take him, by force, from Seth, and it hadn't made a bit of difference. In fact, the pain of failure had almost been more than I could bear. Not only because I had to face the wall of my own limitations, but because it smashed the small yet strong hope that Aaron and I could be, into a small bloody pulp.

"Why do you think Grim can do what you can't?" Jamal asked. He was still in calculation mode, no judgment attached to his words, but they hit me like boulders.

"Jamal," Miranda said in warning, shaking her head.

I've always enjoyed Jamal's inquisitive mind, but his questions were pushing me to the brink.

I couldn't help but pull at my hair in agitation. "Because he will do whatever is necessary to take Seth out."

"Then do that," Jamal suggested quietly.

Another blanket of quiet fell, except for the clacking of Echo's keyboard.

I stared at Jamal, and he met my gaze unblinking. How could he make it sound so simple? How could the logic of it eschew all my arguments to stick to the rules?

My objective was to stay in control of the gods, to punish any who stepped out of line. To protect the souls of the living and the dead. To protect mortals from the machinations of gods.

I had all the power Grim had at his disposal, so him returning would not necessarily yield different results. I hadn't counted on his power. I told myself I counted on his influence, but truly it was because I expected him to return and do whatever it took to win, to assert power.

And if I couldn't do that myself, I was never worthy of the mantle of God of the Dead. I wasn't worthy of Aaron. And he needed me.

As the new logic settled, clicking into place, overriding

my old logistics, my spine straightened, shoulders squaring as a new energy flooded me.

Even as I processed, Aoiki stared at Jamal with something that resembled amazement, as if she was seeing him for the very first time. He blushed under her gaze, putting his attention back on Darth Vader.

"Echo," I said, a new authority in my tone. "Keep looking for Grim, but I need eyes on Seth. I want to know his movements."

A kaleidoscope of possibilities morphed in front of me, patterns arranging themselves into perfect order, illuminating the dark corners where I'd been hiding the truth from myself. My purpose crystallized with such clarity that blue hieroglyphic light briefly flickered across my fingertips.

I knew what I had to do.

The woman paused to grin at me, a terrifying visage if I ever saw one. "Thought you'd never ask."

I was going to throw everything I could at Seth. The only question was, would it be enough to overpower tens of millions of souls of the living?

17

AARON

Seth's face filled every screen on the Strip. Every billboard, every rooftop display, every casino marquee. His teeth glowed so white they looked backlit, which only made the rest of him read like a badly adjusted spray tan.

"Citizens." His voice rolled across Vegas, amplified and theatrical. "For so long, your city has thrived on indulgence. You eat, you gamble, you sin." His tone dipped into a sultry rumble, his eyes practically licking the camera. "You pray at the altar of desire, only to leave empty and yearning for more. I am here to change that. To give you a life of excess, pleasure, spectacle."

A red carpet materialized out of thin air. Literally appeared. It unfurled down the center of the Strip in one long, unbroken ribbon, trimmed in gold. Seth stepped onto it with a swagger so practiced I wondered if he spent time rehearsing in a mirror.

I was a step behind him. Decorative. Silent. A living accessory.

People poured out of buildings as if drawn by a magnet.

They pressed toward the carpet, clapping with mechanical enthusiasm. Their faces told a different story. Confusion twisted their features. Some twisted their arms at unnatural angles, puppets struggling against the unseen force holding them.

Seth soaked it in like it was sunlight.

He touched his chest in mock modesty then tossed a kiss into the crowd. The wave of forced cheering surged louder.

"How can I make this world effortless for you?" Seth crooned. "How can I lift every burden, so you live only in pleasure? All I ask in return is your unwavering devotion. Your admiration. Your appreciation. Your love."

The grin that followed sharpened so much it could cut glass.

He drifted to the edge of the carpet where a line of people clapped against their will. He stopped in front of a couple in their eighties. Their hands smacked together on command. Their faces trembled with fear.

"And perhaps," Seth said lightly, "a few tokens of your affection."

He lifted his hand toward the woman. Her necklace ripped from her neck and shot straight into his palm. She gasped, but her applause never stopped.

The wrongness of everything bit into the marrow of my bones.

Seth glanced over his shoulder at me, reading my expression with smug amusement. "Sentiment holds far more power than money," he murmured. "Mortals used to bring offerings to our temples. We are reviving the old ways."

The crowd cheered again, thunderous and hollow, and I was unable to move, unable to help, forced to watch Vegas become his temple while he paraded me at his side, proof he had already won.

The cheers pounded against my skull in punishing waves. Every clap, every forced scream from the crowd was wired straight into my nerves. I stood there behind Seth, frozen and useless.

I did this. I handed him the weapon he needed. I walked straight into it.

I'd wanted to matter. I'd wanted to be stronger, brave, invincible enough that Timothy wouldn't have to carry the weight of me. I wanted to stand beside him without feeling like a fragile mortal who would crack under the first bad hit. So I let Seth change me. I let myself believe I was taking control of my life. I thought I was stepping into power.

Instead, I'd handed Seth the match and poured the gasoline myself.

Before Seth moved farther down the carpet, his gaze snagged on a girl near the front row. Eighteen at most, flanked by her parents, still clapping against their will.

"Just a few tokens," he murmured.

With a flick of his hand, the girl's spine snapped straight. She jerked forward, ripped from the line, her feet carrying her toward him with mechanical obedience.

"I thank you for such a beautiful trinket," he said to her parents, dripping false sincerity as he inspected their horror-stricken faces.

In an instant, the girl's tank top and shorts shimmered away. A glittering micro dress clung to her body, sequins catching every stray beam of neon. Her ponytail exploded into a sculpted updo, and heavy makeup settled across her features as if brushed on by invisible hands.

Seth didn't stop there. He swept his arm over the crowd like he was selecting hors d'oeuvres. More young people lurched free, their clothes morphing into the same glitzy, hollow glamour. They lined up behind him, each wearing that awful frozen smile the moment resistance flickered in their eyes.

A parade of unwilling offerings.

The cheering spiked again, louder, emptier.

The girl cast one last look at her family. Pure pleading. Then her face snapped back into that plastic smile, and she waved as if she'd always belonged at Seth's side.

Seth basked in it. He fed on it.

And then he turned his gaze down the length of the Strip.

Toward Sinopolis.

A slow, delighted smile unfurled on his mouth. "Time to expand my portfolio," he said lightly. "Why limit myself to the living when the dead are so...ripe for the taking?"

My stomach dropped.

He wasn't just parading power.

He wasn't just taking Vegas.

He was heading straight for Timothy's domain. The souls. The mantle. The seat Grim left behind. If Seth claimed that, he wouldn't just control mortals. He'd control immortals. The balance. Everything.

He had to be stopped.

Before he became the god of the living and the dead.

The ground vibrated faintly beneath my feet. Seth paused mid-stride. His eyes narrowed. He sensed it too.

A hush rippled down the Strip, swallowing even the forced applause. Seth's parade stilled. The neon seemed to dim, as if the city itself was bracing.

I swallowed hard.

"Timothy," I whispered.

There he was, alone in the middle of the road.

Seth turned his head, slow and predatory, toward the direction of Sinopolis...and smiled like he'd just been handed the very fight he'd been aching for.

"Well then," he said. "Let us meet with the scribe."

The carpet surged forward, and Seth led his unwilling procession straight toward Timothy and Sinopolis.

And all I could do was follow, my feet dragging like they'd been filled with concrete, my throat so dry I couldn't swallow, my eyes fixed on Timothy's silhouette as if staring hard enough might somehow make him stronger than a god who'd just snapped the will of an entire city without breaking a sweat.

The carpet glided to a stop.

Timothy squared off in the center of the empty Strip, bathed in the hard glow of neon, as composed as if he were about to begin a lecture instead of confronting a god on the brink of declaring himself ruler of the living and the dead.

He wasn't in ceremonial garb now. No armor. No theatrics.

A simple suit. His tablet in hand. His posture straight, meticulous, deliberate.

Seth slowed, amused. "Well. Look who finally decided to stop brooding and show up."

Timothy didn't rise to the bait. He lifted his gaze with the cool, measured clarity of a man accustomed to sorting the universe into order. "Seth," he said, voice precise, almost gentle. "You have taken power that does not belong to you. You have compelled mortals, stolen offerings, tampered with souls, and violated every law our pantheon agreed to uphold."

Seth spread his arms in mock offense. "Laws are tedious. You of all gods should appreciate efficiency."

Timothy tilted his head slightly. "Efficiency," he repeated. "Yes. And order."

His fingers tightened minutely around his tablet, and it transformed into his staff. "Which is why I cannot allow you to continue."

Seth laughed, loud and delighted. "You? By yourself? Where is your little mortal warrior? Where is the blade that could cut me? You look terribly...unattended."

Timothy's expression didn't shift. Not a flicker.

"I am not here to posture," he said calmly. "I am here to correct."

He took a single step forward, the kind that needed no power display to carry weight. His voice remained level, not raised, but it carried down the Strip with absolute clarity.

"As god of the dead, I am responsible for the balance you have broken. And I will restore it."

Seth's smirk faltered.

Timothy straightened his cuffs, the staff remaining upright on its own. The gesture was somehow more threatening than shouting would have been. It was tidy. Controlled. Final. And absolutely Timothy.

"You will not keep the power you have stolen," he said. "And *I* will stop you."

18

TIMOTHY

"Oh, Timothy," Seth laughed derisively.

"Thoth," I corrected.

The laughter faded from his eyes, though he remained amused.

He wouldn't be amused for long.

I reached into the depths of Sinopolis, into the well of power at the center of Vegas, into the quiet heart of the world where the souls of the dead waited for my command.

The ground beneath us shuddered, a deep, rolling groan that traveled up my legs and into my ribs. Neon flickered overhead, colors stuttering across the blacktop as the asphalt cracked. From the center of Sinopolis, a column of blue light surged upward, clean and sharp, cutting through the night like a blade drawn from its sheath.

Seth's grin tightened.

The radiance rushed toward us, splitting the darkness with a force that vibrated against my skin. Ancient hieroglyphics spiraled through the beam in fluid, looping arcs, then crawled across the pavement in glowing channels that threaded toward my feet. Each one settled into me with the steadiness of old duty pressing into place.

Seth's power answered in kind.

A harsh red burst erupted around him. Snakes of magic unfurled from his shoulders and spine, their bodies formed of shifting scales and heat, each one hissing with the sound of burning sand. The air thickened with the scent of ozone and scorched metal.

Dead versus living. Power against power.

Whatever hold he'd had over the crowd broke, and people ran screaming from the streets. I spotted Xander and Miranda helping people get away to safety. They wanted to face down Seth with me, but I had to do this on my own. I had to be enough, or the gods watching this showdown wouldn't believe in me. *I* wouldn't believe in me.

Our forces collided. A shockwave traveled through the open road with a low, violent crack that rattled windows. My sigils anchored themselves in the air, spinning outward in clean geometric precision. Seth's serpents lunged through them, jaws striking the blue radiance as the two magics ground together in a battle of endurance.

The strain layered through my shoulders and spine, heat gathering at the base of my throat where my power threaded into my voice.

Only then did my gaze shift to Aaron.

He stood behind Seth, a jeweled collar strangling his throat again, the metal catching the red flare of Seth's power. His skin was too pale beneath it. His posture too rigid.

The sight cut deeper than any blow Seth could land.

I felt the weight of what I had not been. The god he needed. The protection he had deserved. The power I had denied myself because I clung too tightly to the rules.

The blue sigils around me brightened, answering that clarity.

The scent of heated pavement thickened in the air. Power thrummed through my muscles, tightening every breath as I wielded more power than ever before.

But even bolstered by the dead, the pressure shifted. Seth's magic surged with the force of the living, millions of beating hearts pouring strength into him. His serpents grew denser, brighter, their fangs lengthening as they fought my sigils back inch by inch. The pavement cracked under the strain. My knees nearly buckled as the living souls he'd stolen bore down on me like a tidal wave.

I whistled low and sharp.

A rumble answered from below the surface, rising in intensity until the ground split along the Strip. Reaper dogs poured out in a rush of motion and shadow, an ocean of sleek black bodies streaked with blue embers. They ran straight into the lines of hieroglyphic light, merging with them, reinforcing the sigils until they ignited with renewed force.

The serpents recoiled as the fused power slammed into them, driving them back in a sweeping surge that restored the balance.

Seth's lips curled. "Calling your pets? Desperate, Thoth."

Assirak appeared at the front of the pack, tail high, eyes bright with purpose. He bounded toward Seth with single-minded determination.

Seth scoffed. "Pathetic. What are you going to do, Thoth?" he asked, tone dipped in mockery. "Overpower me with a bunch of mutts?"

"I'm going to break the rules," I announced, then shot off another whistle.

Assirak leapt.

His bite landed squarely on Seth's balls.

Seth's scream echoed across the Strip. The serpents faltered. The red magic sputtered.

And the reaper dogs pressed forward, their momentum slamming into Seth's power with a force that finally knocked him off-balance.

Snapping out a tendril of hieroglyphs, I used the distraction to send it past Set to wrap around Aaron before yanking him to me. I caught him with one arm.

"I've got you," I said even as I held my power with the other hand against Seth's onslaught.

Seth's cry of fury ricocheted off the buildings even as he threw off Assirak with his power. His normally orange face was red, his eyes bulging as he panted with rage because I took his toy.

That or because Assirak nearly castrated him.

"Bite me," I told Aaron.

Aaron tensed in my hold. Any moment, Seth would compel him with his will. The window was closing fast.

"Now, Aaron," I said, pitching my voice low and steady despite the strain building behind my sternum.

"It didn't work before," he said.

Despite the sweat dripping down my temples, my muscles seizing with the energy it took to control such power, I couldn't help but smile a little. "Seth was more powerful than me before, but not anymore. Because now I've accepted I'd do anything to take you from him. I'd do anything to make you mine. I'd create and destroy stars for you. Which means nothing will keep us from bonding."

Seth bellowed my name, his snakes whipping upward in a frenzy. The air warped around him with heat as he dragged more power from every soul he'd stolen. The pressure hit me like a furnace blast, scorching my blue sigils and sending cracks through the light beneath my feet.

Aaron's mouth tilted up before his fangs sank into my neck.

AARON

Timothy's blood hit my tongue, and it was nothing like before.

No poison burn. No rejection. No violent churn in my gut threatening to hurl itself back out. This was heat and lightning and home, flooding straight into me in a rush that nearly buckled my knees.

Timothy held me with one arm. With the other, he was holding off a god.

I clutched his shoulders, dragging him closer because I couldn't not. Every instinct I had screamed *yes. Mine. Finally.*

The radiance streaming through him sharpened under my mouth, magic flooding my senses. Bitter-sweet, old as the underworld, threaded with something warm that felt like him. Like Timothy. Like the man who straightened his pens and cataloged centuries of history just to feel grounded.

This was nothing like drinking from Seth. Despite needing his blood, there was always an undercurrent of something sour, something wrong. A bond that had been forced.

Seth let out a cry of outrage, hurling another wave of heat that buckled the street. Red serpents lunged, tongues flickering with stolen life.

Timothy didn't flinch.

He angled his body so the blast hit his shoulder instead of me, then snapped his wrist. Reaper dogs answered him instantly, their shadows fusing with his sigils and slamming into Seth's magic with coordinated precision.

And still, he kept his throat tilted toward me.

I growled into him, fingers digging into his shoulders hard enough to bruise. His heartbeat thundered against my lips, each pulse synchronizing with mine until I couldn't tell where he ended and I began. *Mine*, the vampire in me snarled. Mine forever.

Golden threads of light spiraled around us, visible manifestations of our essence intertwining. Each swallow forged our connection stronger, burning Seth's influence away until only Timothy's claim remained.

When I pulled away, having drunk my fill, my fangs buzzed with power and pleasure. I stared up at Timothy with open awe. He was panting, and even as he wielded power with the precision of a warrior, I knew my bite aroused him.

Somewhere across the cracked asphalt, Seth screamed my name as though he still had power over me, but the sound felt distant, thin, unimportant. For the first time since this nightmare bond started, his pull didn't move me at all.

Timothy did.

"How dare you?" Seth roared. "I will take him back. I will make him suffer while you watch." His cool charisma had exploded into an out-of-control rage, and his face was an ugly contortion I quite enjoyed.

"No," Timothy said. "You won't. You may have bonded

him to you, but you could never touch the depths of the connection we share. And now I know power, I—" He faltered a moment. "I never knew it was possible…" His voice was full of wonder. He looked at me as he lifted his free hand. "You make me strong."

The hieroglyphic light spiraling from his skin shifted into a new pattern, ancient symbols burning through the air like molten metal poured into sacred molds. The blue-green radiance deepened to the color of a raging ocean during a storm, so bright it seared afterimages onto my retinas.

A tsunami of raw force gathered height, a wall of divine energy that made my bones vibrate and my teeth ache with its proximity.

Panic flickered across Seth's face.

The ocean of reaper dogs peeled away, clearing the way.

The light slammed forward, rushing toward Seth, but as it neared, it separated into Timothy's tendrils. They sliced through the crimson snakes and right through Seth himself.

With the precision of a surgeon, the tendrils sliced and pulled and cut out chunks of red light from Seth. The red spiraled off into yellow wisps that rocketed away.

Souls. They were souls of the living who'd inadvertently given their power to Seth. I wonder if those people ever felt their absence or recognized the sensation of their souls rejoining with their bodies.

Seth screamed as the magic was cut from him. The sound echoed down the neon canyon and rolled through the city like a dying storm.

Before I could pick my jaw off the ground, I was yanked forward. Timothy's hand fisted in my shirt and yanked me toward him with such force our teeth nearly clashed. His mouth crashed against mine, devouring, claiming. A growl vibrated from his chest into mine as I seized fistfuls of his hair, my nails scraping his scalp. The taste of his blood still lingered on my tongue as I kissed him back with savage desperation, our bodies pressed so tightly together I could feel his heart hammering against my ribs.

When we broke, he was grinning. "I'm sorry it took so long to get here."

A weak laugh escaped me. "I'm sorry I blood-bonded to a douchebag."

"Speaking of the douchebag," Miranda said, walking up from the side, Xander right behind her, "or as I like to call him, the dick pickle." She nodded in Seth's direction.

Timothy released me as we crossed the distance to where Seth now lay. He groaned and mumbled. His skin had grayed and wrinkled as if some of his life force had been sucked out.

"What are you going to do?" Seth spat. "Let your dog behead me?"

"Don't mind if I do," Miranda said, pulling Bob and stepping toward him.

"Miranda," Timothy said, holding up his hand. "I'll handle this."

With an audible *sching*, she re-sheathed her blade with a smirk.

"You can't kill me," Seth coughed. "You don't know how to send me back to the cradle of life. I'm a god like you."

Timothy looked down at him. "You're right. But I'd rather keep you alive, as a reminder to those who might think to cross me. A cautionary tale."

Seth laughed again, but it was less sure this time.

"First, I'm going to take your mind."

The hieroglyphic tendrils unfurled from his skin again, long ribbons of blue-green light that shimmered like molten glass. They drifted toward Seth with calm, deliberate purpose, circling his head until they formed a glowing ring. The light tightened around Seth's skull, tendrils sliding into him with the quiet finality of a scalpel making its first incision.

I watched them thread through the air, the symbols shifting and rearranging as they worked.

Seth's eyes went wide. His breath hitched. His remaining power flared in one last desperate red pulse before the glyphs constricted.

There was no scream this time. Just a shudder. A sag. His limbs loosened and his expression unfocused, as if someone had taken the architecture of his mind and reshuffled all the hallways.

Timothy stepped away, his jaw set.

"What did you do?" I asked quietly.

"I sealed him inside himself," Timothy said. "A mental labyrinth with no doors he can reach. He can think, but he cannot form intention. He cannot plan. He'll never be able to command worship or wield the souls of mortals again."

Seth blinked up at us. He looked even older now. His mouth opened as if to speak, but the words halted halfway, looping back on themselves. "You...you can't...I...I should... we...the...ah...yes...no...yes..." His brow furrowed, a man listening to a conversation no one else could hear.

Nothing coherent followed.

Xander let out a low whistle. "He's like a little helpless baby."

Miranda planted her hands on her hips. "I almost feel bad for him."

We all turned to stare at her.

"What? I said *almost*."

Seth pushed himself up on one elbow, blinking in confusion at the street.

Assirak trotted up to us. Seth startled so hard he fell backward, then stared at the asphalt as if waiting for instructions no one was giving.

Timothy watched him for a long moment, then exhaled slowly. The light around him dimmed to a soft blue whisper.

"He'll live," Timothy said. "But once the others see how I handled him, I don't think they'll be keen to test me."

"Can I just say," Xander held up a finger. "Grim was always a scary motherfucker, but this?" He waved a hand at Seth. "This is scary in a totally new Timothy-patented way."

"Thank you," Timothy said. "I do pride myself on my sense of style."

I couldn't help but grin at that. I wrapped a hand around his waist, near bursting with pride, relief, and not a little bit of a blood buzz.

"What happens to him now?" I asked.

"He needs supervision," Timothy said, leaning into me. "A protected environment. Somewhere secure, contained, and maybe padded. I think we can set him back up at the Menaggio where he can enjoy his life...well enough." Then he turned to me. "More importantly, we can start enjoying our life." His hands framed my face, thumbs caressing my jaw and my entire body tingled with excitement and ached with need for more.

"Oh, I'll make sure of it," I said before our lips met again in a hungry kiss. I paused it only long enough to say, "For all time."

EPILOGUE

TIMOTHY

The leather of the chair creaked under my grip as I tried, truly tried, to maintain some semblance of composure.

The Wolf Town Club stretched beneath the balcony in a wash of colored lights, heat, and bodies. Music pulsed through the floor and into my ribs, steady and relentless, matching the rising tension in my body far too accurately.

I kept my gaze trained outward. Down at the dancers. The bar. The gods lingering on the periphery, watching me the way lesser predators watch a lion at a watering hole. They were deferential. In the weeks since defeating Seth, they had all been filtering into Sinopolis to show their deference. Even if they resentfully did so, I knew they were too scared to cross me now. It benefited them to stay in my favor. To keep the peace.

I should have been assessing them in return. Cataloging alliances. Noting posture and expression. Applying logic to politics.

Instead, all my focus was trained on one thing.

Aaron down below in the VIP box where they couldn't see, his hands braced on my thighs for balance, bucked with every slow pass of his tongue.

I did everything in my power not to move. My fingers curled around the armrests. Sweat gathered at my lower back. Glowing glyphs tickled the ends of my fingertips as the base of my spine tightened.

"Timothy," Aaron murmured, amusement coloring the word, "don't fight it."

Aaron sucked me down his throat so far, I let out a shout. The bass-heavy music vibrated through the floor, mercifully drowning out my cry as his tongue worked the sensitive underside.

"I am not fighting," I said, though my voice was strained as several gods below looked up to catch my gaze. My cock throbbed against the roof of his mouth, each pulse threatening my composure.

Aaron's grip tightened on my hips to hold me still. "You're trying to sit there and act like the respectable god of the dead while I'm doing this. That counts as fighting."

I swallowed hard. "I am attempting dignity."

"Dignity is overrated," he punctuated the point by taking me to the hilt again, his throat constricting around my swollen head in a way that made pre-come leak from me.

My fingers crushed the leather armrests. My pelvis strained upward involuntarily. My head fell back as pleasure surged through me before I forced myself upright, scanning the club with feigned nonchalance while Aaron's mouth devoured me. I cleared my throat to steady myself.

Aaron's mouth was a wet vice, insistent and artful, tracing my throbbing length until delirium bloomed behind my eyes. The sense of being picked apart, blood and thread, was nearly as sharp as the pleasure itself. A bead of sweat tickled down my temple.

"Keep going," I ground out, fingers tunneling through Aaron's thick hair.

Aaron looked up, mouth slick. His pupils were enormous, the blue nearly swallowed by black, like the night sky sucked into a drain.

"Yes, sir," he said, and there was no sarcasm, only smug delight.

His hands slid up and bracketed my hips, his mouth working faster now, lips stretched wet and slick, tongue never letting up. The club crowd heaved with sound and pheromones; the air grew close and laden with ozone and lotus. My vision flickered.

We were out in the open. Anyone could come up here and see what was happening.

But it turned out some rules were more fun to break than others.

Every flick of Aaron's tongue sent electric waves cascading across my skin, driving me closer to the edge.

The tension in my body reached a breaking point, and with a final, desperate cry, I came undone.

Pleasure surged through me, white-hot and blinding, as I spilled into Aaron's mouth. He swallowed every drop, his throat working around me, prolonging the ecstasy until I was shaking and breathless. The world slowly came back into focus, the music and the lights and the distant murmur of the crowd below.

I looked down at Aaron, his lips slick and swollen, his eyes filled with satisfaction and something softer, something that made my chest ache.

He rose with that infuriating confidence he had earned

the right to wield, sliding into the seat next to me in one smooth motion.

I steadied my breath, my hand finding his face with reverence. Leaning over, I kissed him, tasting my essence on his tongue.

"That was incredibly inappropriate," I chided him without any heat.

"Well, what you did when I woke up was inappropriate."

I couldn't help the smirk forming on my face. He woke up with his legs up, me sliding into him, hand fisted around his cock that had hardened in sleep.

He came, fangs deep in me as he drank while I came inside him. A strange circle of life formed between us, though we were both far beyond such things as immortals.

Even as a god, I knew the truth—power could be stolen, worship could vanish, and eternity could unravel faster than a mortal heartbeat. We could lose everything tomorrow.

But as our fingers interlocked, I realized the uncertainty didn't frighten me anymore. I had spent so long denying myself what I wanted, pretending desire was dangerous.

I'd grown so accustomed to the quiet ache of being alone that I mistook it for equilibrium. It clung to me through lifetimes, through empires, through wars no one remembered but me.

Then Aaron walked into my world, a force of nature that dismantled my loneliness with one reckless smile. Immortality had never promised me connection. It certainly never promised joy. Yet here he was, blood bound to me, steady at my side. I realized now the danger was in waiting.

Nothing about the future was a guarantee, but for the first time in ages, I found myself looking forward to it.

~

Visit my website to play catch up with Aaron & Miranda at Perkatory!

You never know what familiar face, or reaper, might join them 😊

https://hollyroberds.com

TASTING RED

Want more of the Hollyverse? Jump from Vegas to a new world in this spicy fairytale retelling!

"Why did you call me here?" I ask, though I know perfectly well why the grizzled old son of a bitch sent for me. I spin the titanium ring around my forefinger with my thumb.

He frowns under his thick beard, across from me at the wooden table. He pushes a pint of ale over before grabbing his own. I don't pick up the mug, but the man shrugs and takes a swig.

How did I end up here? For most ofDear Reader,o consideration for anyone else. Not even the women I sometimes let in my bed. I follow the jobs that bring the most money and that has served me perfectly well until now.

"It's been a long time, Brexley," he says.

Nineteen years, if one were counting. And for nineteen years, I've felt the ghostly shackle, tying me to someone else. Nearly two-thirds of my life, waiting for the shoe to drop.

"Not long enough," I say gruffly, finally grabbing the

mug and taking a healthy swallow of the stuff. I hate to admit the shit is good. So I don't.

I've done everything I could to be free of social ties. There is no place for me among mage, man, or fae. But today is the day my only marker is called.

I owe one being a favor in this entire world and he has summoned me here to the musty backroom of his tavern. Boxes pile high around the room, surrounding us. He named the joint *Sam's*, though his name is Jameson. I never asked who he named it after, and I still won't ask.

The drizzle kicks up a heavy mist that clings to the windows. The cold seeps its way into my bones despite my knit sweater and leather jacket. On a shitty day like this, I'd normally be at home by the fire with a book. But this old son of a bitch has me by the balls.

"You owe me, Brexley," Jameson starts, as if he expects a fight.

I wipe my mouth with the back of my hand. "I'm aware, you old bastard. Just tell me what you want so we can get this over with."

His calloused fingers drum on the manilla folder next to him before sliding it over. "I need you to take care of her."

His tone tells me he doesn't mean take her out for lunch and shopping. He must have been keeping tabs on me to know what kind of business I'm in now. Or maybe he's just a sadistic son of a bitch, and I could be a florist and he'd still give me the same mission.

I push the mug away, despite wanting more. Drinking won't make this problem disappear. But once my only debt is paid, I won't have anything hanging over me. I'll truly be free.

I flip the folder open to a picture and a single page of

details: name, occupation, home addresses. But I didn't need any of that info. I instantly recognize the older woman in the photo. I've seen her many times—on billboards, commercials, packages of food, enamel pins that people stick on their jackets.

A dry snort escapes me. "You've got to be joking."

The old bastard doesn't crack a smile, doesn't move a muscle.

Fuck me.

I run a hand through my already unruly silver hair. "Grandma. You want me to go after Grandma from 'Grandma's House?' The face of the most popular household brand, and one of the most powerful witches known to the world?"

Jameson repeats himself in slow, steady words. "You owe me." Coiled tension is locked up behind his dark eyes and in the set of his broad shoulders. Blood lust shines out from his face. This is business from his past. But I don't ask questions, and I'm not about to start now.

I study him, observing how he's changed since I last saw him. Even more gray strands pepper his black hair and beard. His scowl has only deepened with the years, multiplying the lines at the corners of his eyes. He must be nearing his fifties, but under his flannel shirt vest is a body still packed with the sturdy muscles of a heavyweight boxer.

Once upon a time, I considered this man to be like a father to me. He quickly dispelled me of that notion with an unholy vengeance. He taught me the truth. Dependence is death. Don't buy into the lie. You don't need others to survive in this world. It is a gilded lie that ends with getting stabbed in the back.

Or, in my case, a set of claws raked across my face.

But finally, I'm given the opportunity to dissolve my last tie to another being, and this is my chance. As one of the most beloved celebrity icons, this also may be my chance to get killed.

My fingers wrap around the cold handle of the mug, suddenly thirsty. "She won't be easy to get to. And afterward, I'll be hunted like an animal."

His chair creaks with a loud groan as he leans back with a smirk. I've already accepted his terms. "Good thing you're used to it."

So he does know my business.

I shoot him a cutting look over the edge of the mug as I swallow the rest of the amber liquid.

"After all," he folds his arms across his chest, "you are the Big Bad Wolf."

My grin is half-grimace. "And that is very bad news for grandmas right now."

Head to Holly's website https://hollyroberds.com to find out what happens when Red and the Big Bad collide at grandma's house

LOVE THIS BOOK?

Enjoy more by this author
Vivien woke up with no memories and a terrible thirst for
blood.

The Grim Reaper must destroy all blood suckers.

The reaper dogs just want to get pets and loves in between
fetching the souls for the Afterlife.

*Read this COMPLETE trilogy and you'll laugh, you'll cry, you'll
absolutely die.*

Vegas Immortals: Death & the Last Vampire

*Available on Audio and Kindle Unlimited

WANT A FREE BOOK?

Start your Lost Girls obsession for FREE!
Hooking Tink—my sizzling novella starring Tinkerbell and
Captain Hook—is part of my bestselling Lost Girls series...
and you can download it free right now! Visit my website
https://hollyroberds.com/hooking-tink/ to grab your
copy now!

A LETTER FROM THE AUTHOR

Dear Reader,

Thank you for reading!

HaHA! I told you I would come back for Timothy and Aaron, didn't I? I mean it took 2 years... and y'all were real mad after that bonus epilogue you downloaded from Claiming the Beast...like foaming at the mouth mad. But HURRAY FOR ME!

I'm sooo glad I took my time to write this story because I really needed the whole thing to marinate on the back burner instead of forcing it and then one day, boom, there it was and I set the release date.

I am so grateful for the wild fandom around Vegas Immortals, and while I don't plan to write any more in this series, you never know. I'm essentially a rabid mongoose on crystal meth, so I'm delightfully (or terrifyingly?) unpredictable.

So I hope you follow me to new lands and new series, like the Lost Girls and my uber dark Monster Under the Bed serial to find delight, spice, and new reasons to be upset with me for torturing your sweet little feels. Mwuahaha!

Loved this book? Consider leaving a review as it helps other readers discover my books.

Want to make sure you never miss a release or any bonus content I have coming down the pipeline?

Make sure to join Holly's Hotspot, my newsletter, and I'll send you a FREE ebook right away!

You can also find me on my website www.hollyroberds.com and I hang out on social media.

Instagram: http://instagram.com/authorhollyroberds

Facebook: www.facebook.com/hollyroberdsauthorpage/

And closest to my black heart is my reader fan group, Holly's Hellions. Become a Hellion. Raise Hell. www.facebook.com/groups/hollyshellions/

Cheers!

Holly Roberds

ABOUT THE AUTHOR

Holly Roberds is an Amazon Top 40 Bestselling Author of the Vegas Immortals and Lost Girls series, known for badass heroines, gut-busting laughs, and spicy romance. When not writing, she's playing Dungeons and Dragons, sinking her teeth into her husband's very bite-able arm, or enjoying a "Holly Happy Meal" (prosecco and espresso) at a vibey coffee shop.

For more sample chapters, news, and more, visit www.
hollyroberds.com